We're all a little OVERWHELMED

you are enough

BOOK 1.5

A NOVELLA BY

TIFFANY ANDREA

To all the dogs whose love is so limitless, we feel it long after they are gone.

Contents

This book is an extended epilogue of book one in the "You Are Enough Series", titled We're All a Little Broken. However, I've written this book so it can be read as a standalone. If you haven't read the first book, but would like to, you can find book 1 on my author website via linktr.ee/burdenofproofreading.

All proceeds from this publication will be donated to Carter's Forever Rescue and Sanctuary. They are a no-kill, volunteer run dog rescue doing incredible work. They're funded by donations, so if you'd like to check them out, visit www.cartersrescue.com or visit them on Facebook.

If you're ready, buckle up and enjoy the ride. I hope you find some happy tears along the way.

People like me aren't supposed to get a happily ever after; broken people. I'll never understand how I ended up here. Not physically here. I mean, here, with my family—with a chance at a happy life.

It has been a challenge to adapt to being a wife and mother after spending the last decade in survival mode—alone. I'm not challenged by the time management, nor loving other people; that part is simple. The struggle comes from feeling like I'm failing everyone. Have I taken on too much, too soon, and now everyone I love will pay the price?

That can't happen. I have to figure this out. My family deserves the absolute best, and even though they got stuck with *me*, I'm still going to give them the best I can offer. Anxiety ruled my life for so long, and I'm determined to make sure it doesn't rule anyone else's.

"Good morning, Baby." A voice that is music to my ears startles me. Waking up beside my incredible husband every morning is something I'll never tire of doing.

I lean over to give him a quick kiss. "Bonjour, Mon Coeur." My French accent is atrocious, but it's something that we've learned to laugh about.

Zach pulls the back of my neck toward him for a more passionate kiss. I'm always too self-conscious of my morning breath to go for it, but he never hesitates. I melt into his touch, and for these few moments, I am at peace. When his green eyes stare into mine, I can't think of anywhere else I could ever be happier.

Knock, knock.

"Are you guys awake yet?" Chelsea's shy voice asks from outside our bedroom door.

I begrudgingly pull away from Zach. Chelsea wouldn't wake us if it weren't necessary, and it's a big step that she felt comfortable enough to do so. "Yeah, Chels. What's up? You can come in."

She hesitates to open the door, peeking her head inside before coming in all the way. "Isla came into my room in the middle of the night again. She had a nightmare, so I let her stay." She's staring at the floor, brushing aside imaginary dirt with her foot. "I don't want her to wake up confused, but I can't carry her back to her bed and I have to get ready for school."

I turn to face Zach. I can tell he is disappointed Chelsea's intrusion interrupted our alone time, but he's taken to being a dad like it's as simple as breathing. He doesn't miss a beat before he stands and pulls on a T-shirt. "I'm on it. Thanks, Chels, and good morning." He flashes her his trademark smile as he walks by her. Even from the angle I'm at, only able to see his right cheek, it still makes me swoon.

"Thanks for letting her stay in your room. I know it's probably not very comfortable for you."

Chelsea does not enjoy physical affection, so snuggling is her least favourite pastime. When Isla climbs into bed, she's a heat-seeking missile, headed for the nearest heat source.

"It's fine. I love the little munchkin, so I deal." She shrugs, acting as if it's not an issue.

I get out of bed, sliding my feet into my trusty bunny slippers, and walk toward Chelsea. Nothing would make me happier than giving her a hug, but I'm not sure she's ready for random displays of affection yet. Hugs are few and far between at this stage. I spent years avoiding physical affection myself, so I am respecting her boundaries. "You're a good kid, Chels. I love you."

"Thanks, Zara."

Ouch. She still insists on calling me by my first name, and I've never pressured her otherwise, but I have to admit it hurts when she addresses me in the same way she would a friend. Plus, she has yet to tell me she loves me. I'm only fourteen years older, so maybe it's awkward for her, but I hope one day I can break down her walls enough to help her see that we truly love her. She has deep-seated trust issues and suffers from PTSD after a difficult childhood. She is very guarded.

With her gaze directed at the floor and her hands fiddling with the fabric of her pyjama pants, I get the impression she wants to say something, but can't get the words out. My thoughts race to worst-case-scenario, and I think of all the things she could hate about living here. Her room, her clothing, my incessant need to know where she is at all times, her food choices. The list in my mind is growing by the millisecond.

She breaks me out of my internal chaos that is anxiety. "Have you considered getting Isla a dog?"

That's not what I was expecting. "That... that is actually a great idea. I'll talk to Zach about it, and maybe we can look into some options." I inspect this delicate, freckle faced ginger in front of me and can't help but think her heart is even more beautiful than her outward appearance. "She's lucky to have you, you know? You're the world's best big sister."

"I doubt that. It's just something I thought about while she snuggled into my back last night." She releases a quiet giggle and glances out the window.

"She's tough to sleep with, that's for sure. The few nights she crawled in here, Zach ended up on the sofa because she was laying sideways across the bed. We were trying to all fit, shaped like an H, and Zach got her feet while she used my butt as a pillow." Chelsea and I both laugh at the memory as Zach returns to our room.

"What are you laughing about?" he asks with a smile.

"Just reminiscing about the nights Isla crawled into bed with us and slept sideways."

Zach adds his laughter to the giggle-fest. "I had no idea an eight-year-old child could have such sharp feet. They felt like daggers in my back."

"Well, Chelsea has a genius suggestion." I turn to look at her. "Do you want to tell him your idea?"

"Um… well… I was just thinking. You could consider getting Isla a dog. One that can sleep in her room with her. It might help her feel safer."

Zach takes a second before responding to Chelsea's proposition. "That *is* a genius suggestion." He looks at me. "Why didn't we think of that sooner?"

I shrug. It's safe to say I didn't think of it because I'm terrible at this mom gig. "Maybe we can contact an animal shelter to see if they have any suitable dogs." On one hand, I'm excited about the prospect of a furry creature in the house. Something about having a dog makes a house feel more like a home. On the other hand, I'm berating myself for not thinking of this possibility months ago.

"Okay, Baby. I'll make some calls later today and see what I can find out."

I breathe a sigh of relief when he offers to call because if it were up to me, we'd have to wait a few days while I prepared myself to speak to strangers on the phone. My brain confuses non-urgent phone calls with escaping the jaws of a lion.

"We can keep it a secret until you guys decide. I think she'll be excited, though. She really loves dogs."

"I hope we can work something out. You're right that a dog might help her sleep." I smile at Chelsea and give her a gentle touch on her shoulder. Baby steps. "I'll go make breakfast and leave you two to get ready."

Zach gives me a kiss on the cheek before I exit the room.

Since adopting Isla and Chelsea in March, I've started my counselling services from home. Marketing a counselling business is difficult, and not much fun, so I only have fifteen regular clients. It works well for me to keep busy but still be able to tend to Isla.

A few weeks after we all moved in, Zach and I realized she was struggling so badly in school because of her lack of sleep and social anxiety, we opted to homeschool her. She's thriving in her education, but improving her sleep and anxiety are works in progress.

As I'm in the kitchen making everyone pancakes, Isla comes trudging down the stairs, rubbing her eyes. "Good morning, Sweet Girl. How did you sleep?" I know the answer to the question, but I always ask.

"Fine. Daddy woke me up when he carried me back to my bed."

I laugh because she appears offended he had the audacity to carry her back to her own bed. She's still a tiny girl, weighing in at only fifty pounds, but when she's asleep, she's like trying to carry a dead body—not that I would know about carrying dead bodies.

"I'm sorry. Chelsea didn't want you to wake up confused, so Daddy carried you back to bed. Are you hungry?"

"For pancakes, I'm always hungry." She makes a melodramatic slurp sound, and my heart warms seeing that she's got an appetite again. For the first few months after moving in, she was barely eating. Her body adjusted to surviving on the little she was given in her foster home, so for weeks after moving in here, she couldn't stomach more than a few bites at a time. It still makes my entire body tense in anger at the thought of what Isla's former "foster parents" put her through while she was in their care. Miss Brenda was nothing more than a greedy monster, using Isla to collect the associated income. My momma-bear instincts go into overdrive thinking about the situation.

Once Isla has filled her belly, we go back upstairs to get dressed for the day. Both girls are independent, so we've lucked out by skipping the newborn phase and terrible twos. I'm far too anxious to care for a newborn—I can't even hold one. Second-graders and high-schoolers are more my area of expertise. Well, I am an expert in nothing, but this age gives me less opportunity to screw up. I hope.

After seeing to one of my regular clients, I'm in my office doing paperwork when my cell phone lights up with a call from Zach. "Hey, Handsome. How's work?"

"I wish I was home with you instead."

"Oh, please. Anywhere is an improvement over being stuck with me."

"Baby, are you ever going to believe how much I love being around you?"

I can't accept his words as truth even though I trust him not to lie. It's a predicament. He's honest. My brain is a liar. Yet, I always believe whatever my brain tells me. "Anyway…" I sidestep that whole unnecessary conversation.

"So Carter's Forever Rescue and Sanctuary has dogs up for adoption on their website, so I called to speak with a woman named Lucia. It seems like a good place to start our search. They operate completely with volunteers, so all the proceeds go to helping animals. I really like their mission."

"That sounds good. If we don't find the right dog, we can still donate to them. It sounds like they do outstanding work."

"Sure, Baby. There's an application online we have to fill out, then they'll set up a time for us to come see the dogs they have available. Can you fill it out? Or I can do it later. I'm swamped right now."

"Of course. I'm not doing anything important right now, so I'll get it filled out and hopefully we can set an appointment for this weekend." I hope this application doesn't ask if you've ever killed anyone. That would be a red flag for Carter's Rescue.

"That sounds perfect. We'll have to explain to Isla we will not come home with a dog the same day. We have to go through the process, even if we find the perfect dog."

I respond with a giggle of my own. "You think you're going to tell her no? She could ask you for a horse and you'd be riding one back home."

"A horse? Are we getting a horse?" Isla inquires as she peeks her head in the office.

I pause, hoping she hasn't been eavesdropping on mine and Zach's conversation. That would ruin the surprise. "No, we are not getting a horse. Daddy and I were just joking. Go find yourself a snack, okay? I'll be out in a second."

Zach releases a breathy sigh. "Oh, gosh. I thought I was going to have to get her an actual horse. Thanks for deflecting that. Did she hear anything else?"

"I don't think so. She gave up too easily. But she won't die if you tell her no sometimes. It's okay—even necessary."

"Yeah. She's just been through so much, and she's such a sweet kid. I don't want her to feel neglected ever again."

"I get that. But I draw the line at a dog, okay? I am not shoveling horse poop from the yard."

Zach's boisterous laugh reverberates through the phone. "Well, all right then. No horses. I better get back to work. See you in a few hours. Text me if you want me to pick up anything on the way home."

"I love you."

"I love you too, Baby."

Isla is eating an apple with peanut butter when I enter the kitchen. She's beaming with excitement, and I hope she hasn't overheard our conversation. The element of surprise for her is making this even more exciting.

"Why are you so happy?"

"I was just thinking about horses." She gives me a smile without turning her head, so it appears as a sideways smirk. Chelsea pulled Isla's blonde hair back into two French braids— a style she wears often. Her blue eyes look both angelic and mischievous. Regardless of their intention, I'm a sucker for them. Always have been.

I know how to interpret the look she's giving me. "We are not getting a horse. I hate to break it to you. Don't go getting any ideas of asking Dad because we agree on this. No horses."

"Ah, man. You can't blame a kid for trying." She chuckles, and the sound has me ready to trot down to Horses 'R' Us. How does she do this?

"No, I don't blame you, but it's not happening."

Isla ventures off a few minutes later to tend to the rest of her school work. I return to my office and struggle to stay focused the rest of the day after filling out the online application. It says they take up to forty-eight hours to respond and not to call in the meantime, but part of me just wants to send a follow-up email to make sure they got the application.

No. Resist the urge to be an annoyance and allow the people do their work. The system is working for them, so just follow the rules and wait.

Waiting is so hard sometimes. I want to plan for the day we go to the shelter and be able to order all the items we'll need for a new dog. We have to get food, dishes, leashes, a harness, a collar with a tag, a bed, brushes, and toys. We required fewer things when we adopted two human children. Not that I mind at all; I want to be sure we have everything in time, but not get it too soon and end up spoiling the surprise for Isla.

The possibility of adding another member to our family is so exciting. I always wanted to be a stay-at-home dog mom; now is my chance. Poop-scooping duties aren't too thrilling, but maybe I can practice my puppy-dog eyes and get Zach to do it. He does the yard work because I am not cut out for physical labour. It's a fair trade considering I wash his underwear.

We'll need supplies, so I check out the website for *Mullen's Pet Market*. I can add everything into my online shopping cart and order it when the time is right or go pick it up from the store another day. Oh, we need a pooper-scooper. Zach will thank me for that.

By the time I finish adding everything into my cart, I've tentatively spent several hundred dollars. I just can't pass up the stuffed avocado toast or the cute "I love dogs" mug. And who can say no to a macrame leash with tassels?

My excitement is growing each moment I think about having a fur-baby in our home. My childhood dog, a chocolate lab named Mr. Brown, and I created memories that are highlights of my childhood. I'm so excited for Isla and Chelsea to have that experience, too.

As promised, the volunteers at Carter's have gone through our application, viewing the photos of our house and yard we sent as requested, and have set up a time for us to come meet the dogs up for adoption.

When Saturday morning arrives, I go into Isla's room to wake her up; but she's not there. I walk across the hall to Chelsea's room and see she's wide awake but stuck under Isla's sleeping body, with her hair strewn across Chelsea's torso. Conveniently, she doubles as a heat source and pillow.

"Are you all right, Chels?" It's hard not to laugh.

"I'm fine, but I'd like to use the bathroom and I'm stuck."

Now I can't hold back my laugh. "Sorry, Chels. I came to wake her up anyway, so you can poke at her until she gets off."

Chelsea gives me a weak smile and starts poking her little sister in the ribs. "Isla. Isla. It's time to get up."

Isla lifts her head and grumbles, "No. It's Saturday."

Chelsea drops her head back to the pillow in defeat. She gives up too easily. This little blonde-haired, blue-eyed, sweet talker has the rest of the family wrapped around her finger.

"Isla, wake up. We are going somewhere and it's a surprise."

That child pops up like the bed is on fire. "Surprise? Tell me. Tell me. Tell me! Do you know Chelsea? What kind of surprise? Are we getting a horse?"

You'd never know she has severe social anxiety by the blabbering she does when she's excited. It makes me so proud of her progress that she's gotten comfortable in her new family arrangement so fast. There were obvious challenges in getting adjusted, but we've come together as a unit pretty well.

"Chelsea is coming too. Get cleaned up and dressed, and we'll go for breakfast first."

As Isla runs out of the room, giving neither of us a second glance, Chelsea looks at me and says, "Thanks. I've had to pee for over an hour."

I laugh. "Between you and Zach, she is so spoiled."

It's funny, but it worries me she'll grow up as an entitled brat who thinks she should always get her way. Does parenting ever get easy? Is there a mathematical formula for the perfect balance? I don't know what I'm doing. I'm just loving them, but I am so overwhelmed sometimes.

sla rushes to get herself cleaned up and dressed. She's asked an estimated twelve hundred questions so far this morning, and that number will probably triple by the day's end.

After our breakfast at *Mom's Home Cooking* in town, we climb in Zach's SUV to drive to the animal rescue. I am trying to contain my excitement, but I'm just as excited as Isla. There are few things that make me as happy as doggy kisses, and it's been so long since I had a dog of my own.

As we near Carter's, Isla is taking in the surroundings. She hasn't said a word, which is as much a surprise to me as our destination is to her.

She breaks her uncharacteristic silence as she leans with her face pressed against the window. "What is this place? A puppy zoo?"

Zach, Chelsea, and I laugh.

"Well, it's home to a lot of dogs, but these dogs want to find families to go home with." Zach is the first one to recover from laughter to answer.

Isla's eyes light up. "Are *we* going to give a dog a home?"

"Well, some dogs that come through rescues have been through some tough things, and they're scared too, so we have to find the right dog that will feel safe with us, okay? We might not find one today."

"We're getting a dog? Chelsea! Did you hear that? We're going to get a dog!"

"I heard, Troublemaker. Maybe not today, though. We'll at least get to see some cute dogs. Be careful around them, okay?"

"Okay. Will you stay with me?"

Chelsea hesitates. I know she's going to be nervous here. "I'll try. Let's go see some puppies."

We're greeted at the entrance by a volunteer named Melonie who helps run the rescue. She has a wide, cheerful smile, making us immediately feel welcomed.

As a family, we have yet to decide what type of dog we are looking to adopt. I'd prefer a cute little dog that doesn't shed. Chelsea is completely silent and gives no input. Zach wants a large mastiff, or other "manly" dog. Isla will take anything with or without fur. We settle on meeting the dogs they have available and seeing if we connect with any of them.

We walk through the rescue, and I can see Chelsea is on edge, but she holds Isla's hand like she said she would. I'm so impressed by her natural ability to take on the role of a big sister. At nearly sixteen-years-old, Chelsea is almost twice Isla's age, but they've developed such a love for each other. I have no regrets about our decision to adopt them both.

Isla gushes over the few dogs we've passed by and moves on—though I'm sure she'd gladly take them all home if given the opportunity. We spot a brindle mastiff named Toby, and it seems Zach is in love with him. He's a big, slobbery dog with a handsome face and pleading eyes. I find myself drawn to him too, but Isla wants to look at every available dog before she commits to spending time with one. She's taking this very seriously. I am holding back the urge to bust out the ridiculous baby talk for every creature with sad looking eyes. It may be more of a challenge to restrain myself than Isla.

In the large outdoor fenced area, we spot a fluffy German shepherd sitting in the corner, separated from the other dogs, looking nervous. Melonie informs us the dog is approximately six months old but came in as a stray two months ago. He is still nervous around people. I feel so bad for the poor thing, he nearly brings me to tears.

As Isla approaches the fence, the dog seems to be interested in her. He has a dark snout, with the rest of his hair a beautiful caramel colour, aside from the dark tips on his ears and black saddle-shaped patch on his back.

At that moment, given what we've been told, I assume he's interested in eating her face. I caution Isla, "Be careful, Sweet Girl. He's nervous."

"I know Mommy. I think he's like me."

"What do you mean, 'like you'?" Zach asks.

"He's nervous around new people, but he really just wants someone to love him."

I'm taken aback by her response, thinking that's a very insightful response for a young girl, but she is probably right. As a product of the foster system, Isla has some insight into this dog's emotions that most people wouldn't have.

The nervous dog walks toward the fence, staring at Isla with his warm brown eyes. Something amazing then happens—he wags his tail. Against my better judgment, Isla reaches her hand up to the chain-link fence, allowing the dog to sniff her. He gives her a thorough investigation, and once he's satisfied with her scent, he sits in front of her, staring at her face.

"Wow. I've never seen him have that kind of response to anyone! He's a sweet boy, but he is very anxious." Melonie is glancing between Isla and the dog named Moose, taking in this moment.

As I look up at the information posted on the fence with the dog's name, breed information, and a bit of his history, I notice his birthday. It says estimated birthday March fifteenth—mine and Zach's wedding day. I nod to him to look at the sign and his eyes light up, immediately recognizing the significance.

"Who's a good boy?" Isla sings at Moose. The dog responds in kind by wagging his tail, as if he's accepting her as his person. Isla's tiny arm slips through the fence, and Moose gives her kisses, then rubs his face on her hand.

Melonie stares, awe-struck by the dog's behaviour, given how nervous he had been since arriving. She disappears for a moment and reappears with a leash. "Would you like to take him for a walk?"

"YES! YES! YES! Daddy, please? Please, can we take him for a walk?" Isla knew who to single out to guarantee a yes. Little did she know I wasn't going to say no, either. I was watching a special connection form in real-time, and I was not about to deny that.

"Yes, but I think it's best if I walk him, okay? He's a little big for you to walk yet."

"And you have to calm down. He might get nervous if you're too excited," I add.

"Okay." She takes a deep breath, then turns to Moose. "Are you going to be the goodest boy? I know you are. You're my very best friend in the whole-wide world."

I'm standing a few feet back, trying to hold back my tears. I was unprepared for how emotional this process would be. Seeing Isla so happy makes me elated. I'd say pleasantly surprised, but she has such a kind heart, I'm not surprised.

Melonie moves forward to open the cage, attaching the leash onto Moose. He is just as excited as Isla and comes galloping out toward her. She kneels on the ground, letting Moose come and jump all over her, licking her face, wagging his tail. Her giggles are the most beautiful sound I've ever heard. I think we've found our next family member.

A Girl's Best Friend

4

We take Moose for a walk to McKay Lake, laughing and smiling so widely, I'm feeling cheek pain. Moose and Isla bound along the side of the road, so happy in each other's presence. You'd never know what either of them had been through in their lives. In these moments, they display only joy. They found a kindred spirit in each other, bonded from the moment they met.

I speak with Zach as we're walking. "Well, that was easier than I thought. I think we've found her a dog."

His smile broadens, causing creases around his eyes. When he smiles like that, I fall in love with him all over again. "I don't think we could separate them if we tried."

At those words, I realize we can't just pay for the dog and take him home. We have to go through the adoption process, and it could take a few days before we bring Moose home—assuming we are allowed to at all. Other people could have filled out applications for him, and then it's left up to the volunteers to decide who is the best fit for the dog. As much as I'd like to think no one could have a better bond with Moose, it's not my decision, and I am hardly objective.

I panic at the thought of having to tell Isla she can't have this dog—this dog worked his way into her heart the moment they laid eyes on each other.

It's difficult for me to rein in my running anxious thoughts and focus on enjoying the moment, hoping everything works out for the best. Making that effort is tremendous progress for me. Zara from a year ago would have gone spiralling into panic with no rational thought. I take a moment to be proud of myself for my growth, mentally patting myself on the back.

"What do you think, Chels?" Zach interrupts my internal praise-party and I realize I haven't checked in with Chelsea since we started our walk. Now it's time to berate myself for being a failure of a mother to this impressionable young teen. Mental praise deleted.

Will this ever get easier? Will there ever be a time when I do something right? Am I even capable of doing the right thing, or is my life just going to be one long run of trying and failing?

"I think the dog decided and none of us have a say." Chelsea's shy smile does little to squash my fears of failing.

It should have occurred to me to ask her opinion before we agreed to anything. Her feelings matter as much as anyone else's. I never want her to think they don't, or like she's a second-rate citizen in our family. Could I be any worse at this? My shoulders droop, and my facial expression falls. I'm never going to be good at this mom stuff.

"Hey." Zach stops walking. "Chels, why don't you and Isla take Moose down to play in the water a bit? Zara and I will talk things over."

"Okay. Come on Troublemaker... err... Troublemakers," she says, emphasizing the "s". Chelsea takes the leash from Zach's hand and the girls prance along through the grass toward the shoreline.

"What's wrong, Baby? Do you not like the dog?"

"The dog is great. I don't think you could change Isla's mind about Moose's forever home now."

"Why do you look like your entire world just crashed around you?"

I step into Zach and lay my head on his chest, interlacing my fingers behind his back so he can't get away—not that he gives me the impression he wants to. "Why can't I do anything right?"

"What are you talking about? You did nothing wrong. What's going on?"

I stand there, trying, but failing, to keep my tears at bay, explaining to Zach all the fears and doubts that keep coming to mind.

He listens without interrupting me for a few moments before he speaks. "Zara, there is no way to be a perfect parent. If you spend your life trying to be perfect, you're just going to miss out on all the good. You've been an amazing mother to these girls, and really, that love for them started long before the adoption process. Give yourself credit for all the amazing things you've done for them both. You gave them a family, a home, and love—all things they didn't have before."

"But, I—"

"No. Don't 'but' me and tell me all the ways you are failing, because you're not. You're incredible, and all three of us know how lucky we are to have you." He pulls me in tighter, kissing the top of my head with ease given his seven-inch height advantage. "I love you. And to those girls—girls who have been through hell—you were their light on the darkest days of their lives. They love you too."

"But Chels—"

"Baby, no. Chelsea might not say it, but I know she feels it. You know she struggles to let people in." He lifts his hands to hold either side of my face, tilting my gaze to meet his. Those eyes never fail to make me lose all sense of time and space. "Let's go see how our girls are doing with the dog, eh?"

"Okay." I take his hand and we walk side by side to see *our girls* running along the edge of the lake, laughing and smiling—looking as if they'd never had a hard day in their lives. They appear so full of joy, I think I might burst at the sight. This little Moose is going to fit right in.

I watch as the dog, in its awkward teenager stage, gallops along beside Chelsea, chasing Isla. He jumps up at her playfully, his ears as animated as Isla's face. One ear up, one out to the side, gives his otherwise intelligent face a dopey appearance. He looks like he's having the best day of his short life too—which he probably is.

"We should take Bond back now before they think we dog-napped him," Zach says at a volume our giggling girls can hear him.

"Bond? Who's Bond?" Isla giggles, not breaking eye contact with the furry man of her dreams—assuming she had pleasant dreams.

"Oh, sorry. I mean Moose. We have to take Moose back before they think we dog-napped him. I was thinking something else when I said Bond."

"What were you thinking about, Daddy?"

"I was just thinking about how you guys seem to have such a good bond already. Then I was thinking about James Bond, and Moose here seems to be a ladies' man."

"What's a ladies' man?" Isla tilts her head, looking at Zach.

"Oh, uh. A ladies' man is uh..." He's flustered.

"A ladies' man is someone who likes a lot of girls." I jump in to give Isla an answer, knowing she is not the type to let things go.

Isla giggles again as Moose licks her face. She's seated in the grass, so he only has to stand in front of her. His spit-shine doesn't cause her to flinch or try to make him stop. She embraces the dog-slobber face wash. "I love you too. You're my best friend."

Zach and I look at each other, understanding what is going to happen when we walk the dog back to the sanctuary.

As we walk back toward Carter's, Isla is holding the end of Moose's leash, and he's trotting along beside her as if he's found his place in the world. We walk alongside the fenced-in areas outside and you can almost see the swagger in his step like he's saying, "Eat your heart out. I got me a human." If only it were that easy.

I respect the adoption process, but at this moment, I'd pay any amount necessary to not separate Isla from her new best friend. She wasn't even this happy when we told her *she* was being adopted. We just have to respect the system the experts have in place and trust that they will make the right decision for Moose. It's hard to imagine any other home would be as good for him as ours, but we'll have to wait to see how the situation unfolds. Though, this is the most worried I've been since the girls' adoption approvals went through.

When we return and find Melonie, she asks how our walk went, and if Moose behaved himself.

"I'm going to name him Bond," Isla declares.

"Bond? Like the spy?" Melonie's smile gives me some hope that she recognizes how in love Isla is. I hope she sees that it's reciprocated, too.

"Daddy said he's a ladies' man."

"Uh, I was talking about how he had such a good bond with Isla." Zach looks embarrassed, but Melonie just laughs.

"Well, should we go put Moose back inside?" Melonie reaches to take the leash from Isla.

Isla pulls her hand away, clenching the leash in her little fist. "He doesn't need to go in there anymore. He can come home with us now."

We should have made it more clear to her before we arrived that we wouldn't be bringing the dog home today. I can see why she'd get her heart set on taking her new best friend home and not want to leave him here—even if it is a beautiful dog haven.

I crouch down to meet Isla's eyes, and Moose/Bond jumps up with his front paws on my knees so he can lick my face, too. Thanks, Buddy. That was very thoughtful. "Sweet Girl, we talked about this before. Remember, we said we might not find a dog today? We have to give the volunteers a few days to decide if we are a good fit for Moose."

"Bond. His name is Bond. And no one else will love him as much as I do. I promise." Tears stream from her eyes, plunging a dagger into my chest. "I promise I'll love him so much, and I'll make him the happiest dog in the world. I promise." Her powerful sobs and heaving shoulders are making this even more of a challenge than I thought. We brought her here thinking it would make her happy, and now we have to leave with her heart broken. I want to make this right, but I have to make her realize that we have to follow certain protocols, even when they're hard.

"Isla, leaving Moo… Bond here doesn't mean we won't be able to take him home soon. We just have to follow the rules they have here, and trust that they will make the right decision for Bond, okay?"

Zach leans down to pitch in, but I'm holding my breath waiting for him to offer to buy the shelter just to get her the dog. "Mom is right, Kiddo. I know you love him and feel sad to leave, but they take good care of him here. He will be fine. Hopefully, they decide we can adopt him, and we'll be able to take him home in a few days."

"I promise I will." Isla turns to Melonie with pleading eyes. "Miss, I love him so much. Please let me adopt him."

Melonie appears a little sad about the situation too.

I don't want to put her on the spot, feeling as if she has to confirm we can adopt him or break Isla's heart. "Melonie can't make that decision right now, Isla. Remember, we just have to wait a few days while they go through the process. We'll make sure we have all the dog stuff he'll need and hope we can bring him home in a few days, but if not, we'll find another dog you'll love just as much."

"No, we won't. He's my very best friend, and I'll never love another dog as much as him. I just know it."

I chalk off the comment to her being dramatic, but I know in that little eight-year-old mind, he's become the centre of her world in the last seventy-five minutes. We should have prepared her better. That would have been more sensible than surprising her because she would have had the change to brace herself for leaving the dog here. I really can't get this mom stuff figured out.

As I look around, I notice Chelsea is back over at the car, leaning against the side, wheezing. Now I've been so focused on

Isla, I've neglected Chelsea again. How can I possibly be this hopeless? I'm just failing these beautiful girls left and right.

"I'll talk to Isla. You can go check on Chels." Zach gives me a gentle smile, apparently understanding what I was thinking.

I leave Zach and Isla to sort out the big emotions her little heart is feeling, but confident in Zach's ability to do so. After all, he raised his sister from only a little older than Isla, and she's turned out to be a wonderful young woman. Our girls are lucky to have him as a father figure—I only wish I could be in the same class as a mother.

"Sweetheart? What's wrong? Are you okay?"

As I approach Chelsea, leaning against Zach's silver BMW X3, she turns to face the car, putting her hands on the hood as if she's about to be searched. She's hunched over and doesn't respond.

"Chelsea? What's wrong?" I pick up my pace to reach her. She's crying but attempting to hide her face. I reach down, placing my arm under her chest and lift her to stand. I wrap her in a hug, afraid of how she'll react, but in this moment, whatever is wrong, she needs to know she's safe and loved.

"Oh, Sweetheart. I am so sorry. We shouldn't have brought you here." I cradle her in my arms and breaths slow. How do I keep getting everything wrong? I don't understand how a person can be so inept and clueless to keep making one mistake after the next.

"I'm… I'm okay. Sorry. I'm just being dramatic. I screw everything up." Chelsea pulls herself away from my embrace and steps a few feet away.

"You haven't screwed anything up. I knew this would be hard for you, and you were so brave to come along. Don't feel bad that it triggered some terrible memories. Just remember, you're safe now."

She takes a steadying breath. "I know. I'm sorry."

Zach and Isla walk over to join us. Isla's face is red and puffy from crying, and her ordinarily bright blue eyes are bloodshot. She runs over to wrap her arms around Chelsea's waist. "Are you sad too, Chels?"

Chelsea hesitates. "Yeah. Are you going to be okay, Troublemaker?"

"I'm sad. I miss Bond, but Melonie said she will recommend, whatever that means, that we get to adopt Bond, and Daddy said we can go buy stuff for him. So, you don't have to be sad. It will be okay."

Chelsea's lips turn up into a weak, tight-lipped smile, but it's all I need to breathe a sigh of relief. Maybe we'll survive the day after all.

Our drive home is quiet—an unusual scenario with Isla in tow—but it gives me time to contemplate the day. I think about what Zach said: if I focus on being perfect I miss the good, so I spend the fifteen-minute drive home recalling all the beautiful moments of today. Moments that I don't want to lose in the sea of ones where things went wrong. It may not have been a perfect day, but it was still a good one.

After walking my regular Tuesday morning client out, my phone rings, so I run back to my office. I hate answering phone calls, but it's a necessary evil that comes with running an at-home business.

As I lift the receiver, I'm out of breath. "Zara Haynes."

"I'll never tire of hearing you say that name. Why are you out of breath, Baby?" Zach's deep voice travels through the receiver and lowers my heart rate. His ability to calm me is one of his superpowers.

"Oh, it's you. Sorry, I was walking a client out and had to run back to the phone."

"It's thirty feet." He chuckles.

"Thank you for reminding me how out of shape I am, but I'll have you know I'm out of breath from panicking, not from running!" The giggle escaping made the indignation in my voice far less intimidating.

"We got the call."

"The call?" I ask for confirmation, but I know he means *the call.*

"Yes, we have been approved. We can pick him up Thursday between ten and three."

I let out a cheer but immediately silence myself, not wanting Isla to hear me celebrating. Zach and I discuss logistics of getting a new dog for a few minutes before agreeing to sort the rest when he gets home.

Isla is going to be thrilled, but I don't want to spoil the surprise this time. Nothing can go wrong now—the dog is ours. The big steps are done; now we just need to go get our dog.

A moment later, the phone rings again. Assuming it's Zach calling back, I answer with an abrupt, "Did you miss me that much?"

"Yes, I really did!" my best friend Quinn squeals through the receiver.

"Hey, Amiga! I've missed you, too. How are you?" The smile that was already on my face grows twice as wide. I've missed my best friend so much.

"Gigantic, and hot." Quinn is six months pregnant with her first child. I didn't think it was possible for her husband Tyler to love her more than he did, but he's been doting on her, not wanting her to even sweep the floor—she's not complaining.

We talk for half an hour and Quinn asks me to host their baby shower, since our home has the most space. Of course, I agree, even though I'm the worst party host in the history of time. We schedule a date just over two weeks away so everyone can travel before the snow arrives.

I must have a suspicious smile because Isla walks into my office and hops up in the chair across from my desk. "Why are you so happy?"

She startles me back to reality, and I struggle to find the right thing to say that sounds convincing, but isn't a lie. "Um…

I… uh… I had a good session with my last client. And I just talked to Quinn on the phone. Did you get all of your schoolwork done?"

"Mm-hmm. All done."

For the rest of the afternoon, I keep Isla distracted so she won't ask me countless questions. I'm afraid if she gives me her puppy dog eyes, I'll cave. She helps me make dinner—cauliflower curry. She gripes about the "smelly stuff"—garlic, onions, ginger, and other spices, but she does her best to help.

When Chelsea arrives home from school, she says little and goes up to her room. I've been worried about her since the weekend. I decide to finish making dinner and give her space, but plan to have a chat with her once Zach gets home.

He arrives a short time later, just as Isla and I finish up the rice. He walks in the door and excitement floods through me. I think about how tomorrow will be the last time he comes through the door without a puppy ready to greet him. Now I won't be the only one watching through the window with my nose pressed against the glass as it gets close to Zach's home time. Though, I do not wag my tail.

He strides across the open concept living area to the kitchen, where he picks me up, spins me around, and plants a passionate kiss on my lips.

"Ew. That's so gross, Daddy!" Isla shields her eyes from the offensive action, but she giggles just the same.

Zach places me back on my own two feet, gives me another quick peck, then spins on his heel to chase Isla. "You're next, Kiddo."

Her laughter fills the entire main floor of our home, and I pause for a moment, being grateful for the life we've built. It may have happened quickly, but I don't regret it for one second. Our two girls and that wonderful man make every day better.

Speaking of two girls, I need to check on the second one. I holler at Zach, so he can hear me over the rambunctious giggles happening, to let him know I'm going up to speak to Chelsea. He nods, furrowing his brow, but I respond with a gentle smile and a nod of my own.

I knock on Chelsea's open door to alert her to my presence. She doesn't have any reaction to me entering her space. She doesn't lift her head to look at me, nor does she greet me. Her beautiful copper hair looks as if it's swallowed her head whole when she leans down at her desk.

Her bedroom is white and bright, but she appreciates the clean look. She's very tidy and takes immaculate care of her space. It was Zach's sister Jasmine's room before she moved into her own place in Toronto to lessen her commute time to college, so it's beautifully decorated and Chelsea didn't want to change anything when given the opportunity.

I walk over to the ottoman, which matches the armchair by the window, and take a seat. I'm a few feet away from Chelsea, who's seated in her wheeled office chair. She still hasn't acknowledged me, and I'm growing more concerned.

I clear my throat and say her name, but she still doesn't reply. Now I'm bordering on annoyed because there's no reason for her to be rude. "Chelsea!" I shout, this time reaching my hand to tap her shoulder.

She jumps out of her chair fast enough you'd think it turned to lava. She spins to face me, removing her ear buds connected to her phone. "You scared me!"

Whoops.

"I'm sorry, Sweetheart. You seem to be having a tough week, so I came up to talk to you. I knocked and called your name, but I guess you didn't hear me." I point to my own ears to show I noticed the ear buds.

"Oh, sorry. I was just listening to some music a friend told me about."

My eyes shoot open so wide, I could hold them open with toothpicks. "A friend?" Chill, Zara. Don't be *that* mom. Just. Be.

Cool. My excitement builds, wondering if she's found a boyfriend, but then I realize she's far too young and impressionable for that yet. No, just be cool, Zara. Be supportive. "Tell me about your friend."

She spins the chair to face me and takes a seat again. She's twisting back and forth in the chair, wringing her hands, which she repeats while refusing to make eye contact. It hurts knowing she's nervous to talk to me about her friend, but finally she speaks. "He's a guy from school. His name is Liam. I guess he lives close by. He's been really nice and doesn't like the immature high school drama either, so we just kind of... I don't know. We just try to avoid it together, I guess."

I take a moment to process what she's said. Liam, he, together. Breathe. Be cool. "So. Um. This Liam? Do you like him? Like, *like* like him?"

"No. It's not like that. He really is just a friend. I promise. He, um. Well, he just got his driver's license and can drive to school now, so he offered to pick me up and bring me home. I thought that might be easier, so Zach doesn't have to drive me?"

"I'm not sure, Chels. We don't know him. Maybe you can have him come over one day and we can meet him. Then we'll talk about it again, okay?"

Her head drops, but she nods in agreement. Having rules because someone cares about her safety is a new concept for her. Her entire life until now has been rules for the sake of control, or rules for the sake of rules.

"Are you okay otherwise? Are there any issues at school or anything you want to talk about?"

She shakes her head. "No. Everything is fine."

I tell Chelsea that Carter's approved us for Bond's adoption and ask if she wants to take the day off of school to come with us to get him. She declines, and I understand. She follows me downstairs for dinner as a family—one where Isla talks non-stop about the facts she's learned about German shepherds over the past two days. My over-eager student produced an entire report for me, in addition to her schoolwork, with tips and tricks for raising German shepherds. Subtle hint. I can't wait until we tell her we are bringing him home.

Thursday, Zach skips work so we can go pick up the items we need for Bond before collecting him from Carter's. We told Isla when she woke up this morning, and the poor child cried her little eyes out with tears of joy. She's buzzing around the house; her feet and mouth motoring non-stop. Her enthusiasm is contagious, and we're all feeling the excitement of bringing home a new puppy.

Given my anxiety level, I've been researching dog training, proper foods, breed specific information, and anything else I could think of over the past few nights. Thanks to Isla's thorough breed-specific report, I am confident I know enough information to survive the first few weeks of puppy ownership. It can't be that hard, right? Just take him out to pee and feed him?

We climb into Zach's SUV, minus Chelsea because she's at school, and we head to *Mullin's Pet Market* to pick up the dog's necessities. Isla is so excited to pick a few toys and select food for Bond. She's very concerned about getting him the best of everything, and I don't think Zach is going to tell her no.

Once we arrive, Isla zooms off in search of the latest and greatest dog gear. Before I'm fully in the store, she's already picked up a few items of interest.

"Can we get this? And this?" She holds up a massive bone that must be from a dinosaur, and what appears to be a dog backpack.

"Do you really think we need a backpack for him?" I ask, hoping to talk some sense into her and avoid emotional purchases.

"Of course!" She looks at me with her face twisted in confusion.

Why I would question the need for a dog backpack? It appears that in her eight-year-old mind, it's a necessity.

"He'll need a backpack for treats and water when we go for walks. Oh, and a lifejacket!" She buzzes off to find some other items she deems essential for her new best friend, with no consideration for the dollar amount.

I turn to Zach. "We should give her a budget."

"It's fine. Let her get what she wants."

Surprise, surprise. I roll my eyes. "Zach, we can't keep spoiling her. She has to have some limits. It's reasonable to set a dollar amount."

He turns to face me and takes one of my hands in each of his. "Baby, can we just enjoy the process today and not worry about the money or about parenting guidelines? Please, can we just love her and let her be happy?"

I know she can still be happy and have limits, but Zach is a far better parent than I am, so I concede to his request. It's my specialty to consider both long-term and short-term effects of every scenario until I'm exhausted and talk myself out of whatever it was to begin with. Today, I'll try my best to just enjoy the ride.

One hour and $1484.29 later, we've purchased a ridiculous number of items to ensure Bond is the happiest, most stylish pet on the block. Isla picked a handsome tartan collar and a lime green harness for him, along with about fifteen toys, two bags of food, blankets, two dog beds—one for each level of the house—treats, and bowls. I got the macrame leash I had been eyeing online, and Zach grabbed some vitamins and first aid items. He didn't even bat an eye at the cost of everything we picked up. He was happy Isla was happy.

I love that he's so willing to do whatever he can for her, but I worry that she'll grow up thinking this is all normal and all she has to do to get something is ask. To be fair, I worry about everything, and I'd assume I was parenting wrong regardless of how we did things.

We get in the car to drive the fifteen minutes to pick up our new family member and Isla's mouth has not stopped moving long enough for her to intake a full breath. The child is like a diesel engine—once she gets warmed up, she'll go for hours.

As we pull into the facility, the SUV shakes, and not on account of the Muskoka roads. Isla is bouncing in her seat, and by the motion of the vehicle, you'd think she was ten times her actual size.

A different volunteer comes out to meet us, shaking mine and Zach's hands, introducing herself as Lucia. She's the one Zach spoke to when he first called, and it's nice to put a face to the name. The kind looking Italian woman has short, dark hair and a slight frame. She requests we follow her into the office to sign some paperwork before we'll be able to take Bond home, and also pay the adoption fee. I don't think I've ever been so happy to part with money in my life. With us taking Bond, that frees up space and resources for them to help another dog in need, and I can't think of many things more wholesome than that. Dog people are my people.

Once we've done the paperwork, which would have gone faster had Isla not asked so many questions, we make our way to where Bond is waiting. The moment Isla comes into his sight, it is the purest, most touching moment I've ever witnessed.

Lucia informs us that Bond—rather, Moose—appeared depressed over the last few days, but you'd never know now by looking at him. His tail is whirling like a helicopter blade. He's jumping up on the other side of the gate he's behind as if he's desperate to get to his best friend he obviously recognizes.

Isla turns to Zach, then to Lucia with pleading eyes. "Please, can we let him out now?"

Lucia steps forward to release the gate, only enough for her to slide in so she can equip the dog with a leash. During our paperwork signing, Lucia advised us to keep a close eye on him for the first few weeks, not letting him off leash at all until we've established a firm relationship with each other. Dogs that were strays have a higher likelihood of going off exploring. Thankfully, we have a fully fenced yard, so we shouldn't have an issue, but we will heed the advice of the experts. We don't want to put Bond in any danger—he is coming to us to live a long, happy life.

Once we've tied up all loose ends with the wonderful people of *Carter's Forever Rescue and Sanctuary*, Isla takes the handle of the leash from Zach and struts toward the car. It's amazing watching these two little creatures, completely different species, but somehow, they just understand each other. No words are needed when your hearts speak to each other.

Isla is chatting Bond's ears off as he trots along beside her. When they get to our vehicle, Zach opens the tailgate, assuming the dog would go in the back on the bed we purchased.

"Daddy! He can't go in there!" The horrified look on Isla's face is almost humorous.

"Sure, he can. I put the bed down. He'll be comfortable back here."

Isla crosses her arms, leash still in hand. "If he sits back there, then I do too."

"Isla, don't be silly. He's a dog; you're a child. You can't sit in the back. It's illegal." Zach tries to reason with her, and I'm impressed he didn't cave without argument. I guess scratching his leather seats is where he draws the line.

"He's not just a dog. He's my best friend." She walks past Zach, opening the back door, and before either of us can protest, Bond jumps in and sits on the floor on the driver's side.

Zach heaves a sigh, pulling the tailgate down. "If he stays on the floor, he can sit back there. But he has to behave."

"Way to show her, Boss Man." I giggle at Zach. He's a handsome, fit, intelligent man, but he's consistently getting his butt handed to him by an eight-year-old girl.

"I can't argue with her. She's going to be a lawyer." Zach walks toward the passenger door, opening it for me so I can get in. He's never wavered in his gentlemanly ways and while I am not old-fashioned, I adore that he still loves to care for me in these small ways.

Before we pull out of the parking lot, Bond is on the seat behind Zach, adding his slobber artwork to the window. I don't say a word, but I'm giggling at the thought of Zach discovering it later. Aside from not staying where he instructed, which I can't blame him, he was well behaved on the drive home. We may have adopted the best-behaved dog in the history of the world.

It's been twenty-four hours since we arrived home with Bond. I'm not sure I'm going to survive. He's eaten the living room rug, but he'd peed on it already, so it was ruined, anyway. He chewed Isla's soccer shoes, but I think that may have been a conspiracy between them because team sports are not her forte. He ate a box of crayons, and I'm just imagining how that's going to look a few hours from now. He unrolled a roll of toilet paper—which doesn't sound so bad—except it was on the holder in the upstairs bathroom, and no one stopped him until he was in the kitchen. It must be toilet paper designed by a structural engineer because its integrity is first class.

We've taken him on walks, let him play fetch in the backyard, made sure he is going out often, rewarded his good behaviour—we're doing everything the internet articles said to do. Why is this so much harder than I realized? Mr. Brown never put me through this much torment.

On the bright side, I've never seen Isla happier. The two of them have been snuggling on the sofa, watching 101 Dalmatians and Isla mutes the TV when the all-dog alert goes out so Bond wouldn't worry about missing puppies. Bless her little heart. She also slept in her own room last night with Bond on his dog bed beside her, other than when he got up to pee on my bathroom floor. I have to give him credit for choosing the right room.

I've already given up my hope of keeping the dog off the furniture—I suppose it is FURniture. He welcomed himself into the family faster than I thought possible without needing an adjustment period. He just walked in like he owned the place and started with his redecorating suggestions. The first thing to go, our $2000 wool area rug.

I know we'll all need time to get adjusted, and I certainly don't blame the dog for not knowing how to behave in the house because he's never lived in a home aside from the rescue. He can't know what's expected of him until we teach him. Maybe we should have a heart-to-heart.

My cell phone rings, and a handsome blond with green eyes lights up my screen.

"Bonjour, Mon Coeur."

"Hey, Baby. How's it going over there?"

"Do you want the long version or the short version?" I groan but try to keep positive.

"Uh oh. That doesn't sound good. Did he pick up where he left off last night?" Zach chuckles. He chuckles—the audacity!

"It's not funny. Why did he choose my shoe to poop in? I took him outside for twenty minutes!"

Zach is in an uproar on the other end of the phone, and I can't help but laugh along with him. I'm kind of offended Bond chose my shoe to deposit his excrement in, but maybe in his mind it was a gift and he had nothing else to give. Yes, that must be it.

"Are you done yet?"

"I'm sorry, Baby. I just keep thinking about you walking around, ranting about the foul smell and trying to sniff it out like a hound. I'm going to call you Toucan Sam."

"Toucan Sam?"

"You know? Follow your nose?" He laughs again, obviously pleased with himself.

"Aren't you hilarious," I say, my voice dripping with sarcasm.

"Aw, don't be mad. I was actually calling for another reason."

Ambiguous statements are a sure-fire way to amp up my anxiety. "And what might that be?"

"Get yourself ready for six tonight. I'm taking my wife on a date."

"A date? Who will watch the kids? Where are we going? Why are you taking me?" My what-if mentality has every dog in the fight right now, preparing each plausible scenario. My brain decided long ago this process is the most logical, rather than waiting for a simple answer.

"Jasmine will come stay with the kids. The rest is a surprise. Just be ready, okay? I'll be home around 5:30 and I'll get ready quickly."

"Are you sure? That's a long way for Jasmine to come. What if she's missing classes? I don't want her to think we're using her as a babysitter. I mean, Chelsea is nearly sixteen, so she doesn't even need someone here with—"

"Wow. Slow down. Just get yourself ready and trust me to take care of the rest, okay?"

I release a long exhale, conceding to his request once again. He never lets me down. "Okay. Good thing you called early because I need at least that long to look presentable."

"Baby, you're just as beautiful in sweatpants as you are in a gown."

"Okay, Romeo. Cool it on the lines. I already married you." I laugh. He's insane if he thinks I'd believe that. Though maybe I am equally attractive either way—I'm just not pretty, regardless.

There is a loud noise from the living room, followed by Isla's screams.

"I have to go." I hang up the phone while racing to the living room. When I exit the hallway from my office, I notice Bond overturned our end table, and the lamp is now a mangled mess with lightbulb glass shattered.

Dog.

"Isla, don't move from that couch. There's glass everywhere. Let me clean it up."

"But Bond is going to get it in his paws. I have to stop him." She attempts to jump down from the sofa.

"Young lady, don't you move from there. I'm serious!" I speak with a harshness in my voice that I've never used before, and the situation isn't even her fault. Here I am yelling at the child for wanting to protect her dog. What a poor excuse for a human being I am right now. Why am I the least capable mother on the planet? I try to backpedal my words, but the damage has been done.

Isla's eyes are brimming with tears as she stares at me, waiting for me to turn green and rip my shirt off or something. "I'm sorry. Bond is sorry too. I know it."

Worst. Mother. Ever. "No, I'm sorry. That was wrong of me to yell at you. I'm not mad; I promise. I just panicked because I don't want you to get hurt."

After sliding my feet into a pair of sandals, I grab the broom and dustpan, along with a container for the glass shards.

To reassure Isla, I add, "I'll go put Bond out in the yard, so he won't get hurt. You just stay on the sofa until I get the mess cleaned up."

She nods through her tears, clearly still upset by my outburst.

I call the dog, open the door to let him outside, but he doesn't want to go alone. I throw a ball to entice him, but he's not budging. He refuses to go out without his bestie. I grumble because I am frustrated by how stubborn he is. I had no idea he'd come in here thinking he was the boss. "Fine then. If you get glass in your paw, don't say I didn't try to help."

He stares back at me, one ear up, the other flopped to the side and his head tilted. I'm curious what he's really thinking right now. Probably about pooping in my other shoe later—a Crayola rainbow poop.

I walk back into the living room, sweep up the glass, then run the small vacuum around just to be sure. The lamp is a goner, but the table is fine. Another redecorating choice.

Jasmine arrives a short time later and Bond is the first to greet her at the door. She walks in the house looking every bit as beautiful as she always does, and Isla goes running toward her, jumping into her arms.

"Auntie Jas! I got a dog! His name is Bond, and he's a German shepherd, and he's the goodest boy. He's my very best friend and I love him so so so so so so so so much." She got that all out in a single breath.

Jasmine laughs and her facial features remind me of her brother. I welcome her with a hug and thank her for coming. I know it's a ninety-minute drive from her condo, so it's not like she's right around the corner.

We talk for a few moments, but her sibling loyalty keeps her from divulging any information about where Zach is taking me tonight. I decide to trust Jasmine to handle things and just enjoy the evening with my hunky husband. Everything will be fine.

When Zach arrives home at 5:30, I lock myself in our ensuite bathroom and insist he get ready elsewhere, so he won't see me until I'm ready. After some grumbling on his part and me placing his grooming items outside the bathroom door, he submits to my terms.

I've chosen an emerald-green satin slip dress that falls just below my knees with slits up either side. It's far more scandalous than I'd normally consider, but thanks to Spanx, I think I pull it off. My black sling-back heels, leopard print clutch complete my look. I grab a light cardigan to take with me for when it gets cooler this evening. My hair is down in soft curls, and my makeup is simple with my best attempt at a smoky eye. I'm as ready as I'm going to get. Time to go find my man.

Voices travel up the stairway from downstairs, one of which is the deep, dreamy voice of the love of my life. I walk down our curved staircase, which leads into the living room, and as I'm nearing the bottom, I catch Zach's eyes. He starts hacking and wheezing.

I walk toward him, placing my hand on his arm, as he's now hunched over, coughing. I panic he's developed lung cancer or emphysema. "Are you okay? What's wrong? Do you need a doctor?"

He clears his throat and takes in a breath, then stands up straight and looks down at me with the smile that changed my world. "Baby, you look so beautiful; I choked on my drink."

I skip right over the compliment buried in there and zero in on the fact that I made him choke. That's a bad thing. "I should change." I turn to walk back upstairs, but Zach's hand grabs my arm.

"Please don't. You look stunning. I want to take you out just like this." He winks at me, and I am powerless to refuse his wish.

"Oh… okay. If you're sure."

I give Jasmine a quick rundown on dog care, bedtimes, food options, safety protocols, and where things are located. She lived here for five years before I did, so I realize most of the information I provide is redundant, but she understands my anxiety, so she doesn't stop me. I give Isla a quick kiss on the top of her head, and Chelsea a tap on her shoulder, hopeful one day hugging her will be okay. Bond gets a little scratch on the ear, and he's sitting like he's competing at an AKC show. Maybe he's adjusting to civilized life indoors.

Zach and I exit into the garage, and before he opens my door, he spins me around and pulls me in for a passionate kiss. We're still honeymooners, though our married life has been far from traditional. Alone time has been rare, and whenever we do, there's always something serious to discuss. Tonight, I just want to focus on him and me, not worry about anything else going on in our lives. Any issues will wait for after our date.

Zach drives us to *Lighthouse Point Restaurant*. The atmosphere is beautiful, and our table is overlooking the water. Our server, Hailey, is bubbly and attentive, allowing us to enjoy the evening in peace, but still tending to our needs. Overall, the experience was wonderful.

It was a struggle to drive our conversation along without it being entirely about the kids. Because of how quickly Zach and I married, then started the adoption process only days later, we never had a period of adjustment for the two of us. It's as if our entire identity as a couple has been as parents to two girls, each with their own struggles and needs. I don't regret our choice, but it comes with its own set of challenges. Maybe he regrets marrying me or adopting the girls. Oh gosh, now I've gone and added a dog into the mix. He must hate me now.

Anxiety has ruined my appetite. I push the rest of my squash and mushroom risotto around my plate. Maybe if I rearrange it the right way, it'll send me a message. Yeah, sure. Probably, *there isn't mushroom for romance with two kids, so you butternut get your hopes up.*

"Baby, where's your mind at? You look upset." Zach's soft eyes peer at me as he reaches a hand across the table to place over mine.

"I... um... nothing. It's stupid."

"What's wrong? Did you not like the food? Or the company?" He smirks.

"Both the food and company were more than I could ask for. I... I don't know. I guess I'm just wondering if you regret your decision to marry me. You went from bachelor to family man so fast, and I wonder if you resent me for it."

His mouth drops open, and he shakes his head as if he's clearing cobwebs. "Are you kidding me? Not only do I love you more than life, I love our girls, too. I don't know if you've noticed, but even with the chaos, I'm happier than I've ever been."

"You're not just saying that? You really are okay with everything? I'd hate to think you agreed to these things only to make me happy."

"Never. I love you, and I love our little family. We might be unconventional, but I wouldn't change anything." He takes a pause for a moment to browse the dessert menu. "Do you know why I brought you here tonight?"

"I assume you were trying to woo me, Mr. Haynes." I laugh, thinking I am far funnier than I am.

He smiles at my attempted joke. "Well, I enjoy wooing you, yes, but Monday was the one-year anniversary of the best day of my life."

I try to think back to one year ago. "Really? The day you ran me over with your bike is the best day of your life?"

"To be fair, I did not run you *over* with my bike. I crashed into you. But yes, it was the best day of my life. I laid eyes on the most beautiful woman I have ever known, and even though she ran away from me thinking I was a serial killer, I knew we'd meet again. I knew that day would change my life forever."

It still boggles my mind when he calls me beautiful. When he says anything positive about me, really. "Well, I can't say I appreciated your methods, but I can't complain about the results."

Hailey comes to the table to ask if we want dessert, so we decide to share the Earl Grey Crème brûlée. When our dessert arrives a short time later with two spoons, as requested, Zach looks at me so intensely that he makes me feel like the only person in the room. He digs into the beautifully presented dessert, feeding me the first spoonful. He watches my face, waiting for a reaction. This creation tastes divine—dare I even say, more delicious than Oreos. It's probably a good thing for my waistline that I do not possess the skills, nor the patience, to recreate this dessert at home.

As our evening winds down, after using all my willpower to resist licking the residue from our dessert dish, we return to Zach's vehicle hand-in-hand. As per his custom, he stops me to pull me in for a kiss before opening the door. The intimate moment makes me feel loved—something he never fails to do.

Our drive home takes nearly an hour. It's after eleven by the time we pull into our garage. I can hear Bond barking from inside the house. At least he has taken on guard dog duties.

When we walk through the garage door into the house, Zach and I both come to a halt.

"What the heck happened here?" Zach pans the space, taking in the damage.

Jasmine pops up from behind the sofa—rather, what remains of the sofa—with a garbage bag in her hand. There is shredded, yellow cushion foam wall to wall. "Thank God you're home. I went to put Isla to bed, and Bond stayed up to party." She lets out an awkward giggle, but her facial expression turns remorseful. "I'm really sorry."

I turn to stare at Zach. "Well, I guess he didn't like the sofa either."

Bond's redecorating services. Available for hire. Excellent option for anyone who wants to purchase new furniture, but their spouse disagrees.

I t's closing in on one in the morning by the time Jasmine, Zach and I get the main floor of the house clean, but I'm sure we'll be finding foam for a few days. I spent a solid twenty minutes researching online if couch foam is toxic for dogs, and Dr. Google says it depends on how much they have ingested. So now, rather than being annoyed over the sofa, I'm worried Bond will develop an intestinal obstruction. I never thought I would become so invested in a dog's poop before, but here I am, standing outside in my pyjamas, monitoring the dog's every move. No luck yet, so I'll lie awake most of the night stressing over dog poop, or rather, a lack thereof.

When Bond and I return inside, he bolts upstairs, hopefully to go sleep with Isla, and not eat our mattress. Jasmine and Zach are in the midst of an animated discussion, laughing, with tears running down Jasmine's face.

"What did I miss?" I ask, eyes flicking between the most beautiful sibling pair ever created.

"Jas was just telling me about her night and her reaction when she came down to find the couch destroyed."

"I'm sorry for laughing, Zara, but it was just such a shock. The cheeky bugger. He followed us upstairs when it was Isla's bedtime, and I crawled into bed with her to read her a story. I must have fallen asleep for a bit. When I woke up, Bond was in his bed in Isla's room. I thought, 'what a good little doggy.' Then I came downstairs and saw his handiwork. I was just imagining him ripping it to bits, probably trying to teach me a lesson for sleeping in the bed with his best friend. I took his spot." She and Zach are both laughing at the situation.

"Well, he'd already given me his opinion on the area rug, a lamp, a few pairs of shoes, and our choice of toilet paper, so it shouldn't surprise me. I just hope he's okay. It would probably be safer to crate him until he we train him, but I just can't bring a crate in the house."

Jasmine and Zach both look at me, nodding their understanding. We sit around the kitchen island chatting for a while before we all head off to bed. I've missed Jasmine. She's doing so well in her fashion design classes, and while I have no claim to her success, I am so proud of her.

I peek into Isla's room and giggle at the sight. Bond is sprawled out on her bed in the exact middle and she's sleeping in a semi-circle at the head of the bed. For a dog who spent the first months of his life on the streets, he sure is an expert in bed-usage. Hopefully, his skills help her get a decent sleep.

As morning rolls around, I'm awakened by slobber across my cheek and a giggle. I open my eyes and see Isla laughing at Bond's wake-up method. He's turning out to be a full-service animal. Let's hope he's retired from redecorating and focuses on security and sleep assistance.

"Good morning, you two. You're up early." I notice the sun is not fully up, and the sky is painted in an array of pinks and reds.

"Guess what!" Isla's little face beams at me. "I slept all night!"

I sit up as quickly as my unconditioned abdominals allow. "You did? The entire night? No nightmares?"

"I don't think so. Bond woke me up because I think he has to, you know"—she leans in to put her mouth to my ear—"doo-doo."

Doo-doo! Oh! Couch foam! I jump into action, grabbing my bunny slippers and fleece robe. I look every bit the frazzled housewife right now, but I don't care. The dog's got to poop! I run downstairs—more of a slow jog—and open the backdoor to let Bond out. I follow him and stand on the deck, watching his every move. Instead of getting down to business, he deems it necessary to rid our two acres of any free-loading wildlife. Be gone, squirrels and birds.

When he does pause, making me think he's about to do his business, he gets distracted again. The late September morning is cool, and there is a thick dew on all the outside surfaces. I can't sit in the patio chair to wait without getting wet, so I just stand on the back deck, praying for number two. No such luck.

Defeated, Bond and I go back inside, and Isla dishes up his breakfast. She arranges it in his bowl in a way that would make Gordon Ramsey award style points. Bond turns his nose up at it, even declining water.

Isla asked what happened to the living room. She was fast asleep when Bond got to work last night. Zach and I carried the sofa and area rug out into the garage to wait for the next trip to the waste management site, so our living room has only a pair of surviving armchairs and a trio of tables.

"Well, Mister Bond here decided he didn't like our sofa, so he shredded it to bits." I give her an unamused look, but I'm not mad at the dog—and I'm certainly not mad at Isla.

"Bond, that's a naughty boy. You can't eat the furniture! You're going to make yourself sick." Isla is wagging her skinny index finger in Bond's direction as he sits in front of her, giving her his full attention.

"I'm a little worried because I looked online and a few websites said couch foam can cause blockages, so if he doesn't poop soon, he'll have to go to the vet. Especially because he hasn't eaten." As soon as the words leave my mouth, I regret them. Mom of the year, making the kid stress over her dog's well-being.

Isla drops to her knees beside the dog, wrapping her arms around his neck. "Bond, what have you done? What if you have to go to the doctor and they have to cut you open? I don't want you to get hurt." She cries, obviously scared for her bestie. Bond leans into her like he is trying to offer reassurance. For a dog that was skeptical of people only one week ago, you'd never guess now by the way he responds to her.

"Don't panic. We'll get him looked at, and he'll be fine. As a stray dog, he probably ate a lot of stuff he shouldn't have, and he's survived. He's a tough boy."

"I'm going to get dressed so we can take him to the vet." Without another word, she rushes up the stairs as Zach is walking down.

He enters the kitchen where I'm standing after having put on the coffee maker for him. "Thank you, Baby. I woke up and wondered where you were. Did you get enough sleep?" He leans in to give me a good-morning kiss.

"Probably not, but I know you'll share your coffee with me if I need it." I wrap my arms around his waist, laying my head on his chest. My favourite place to be. "I think we need to take

Bond to the vet. He hasn't pooped, and he won't eat. Isla is terrified, so I think we should take him."

"Okay. Just let me grab a quick shower, and then I'll make a coffee to go." After a quick peck on my head, I release my grip on him and he heads back upstairs. His calm demeanour helps relax me a fraction.

I scroll through my phone looking for a veterinary office that is open Saturday mornings. Our best bet appears to be taking him to Gravenhurst since most vets like weekends off. I guess our dog needs to be trained not to eat sofas on Friday nights. That is strictly a Monday to Friday daytime activity.

Once I'm dressed, Zach and Isla declare they are ready as well. We buckle on Bond's lime green harness with the matching leash. I've got his records we received from Carter's. Zach woke Jasmine to tell her where we are going before making his coffee. Now we're ready to go.

This time, Zach doesn't even bother trying to open the tailgate to put the dog back there. He opens the back door for Isla, and Bond jumps right in.

Isla laughs. "He thinks he's a people."

I laugh. Zach doesn't. He's not particularly fond of his vehicle, in the sense he doesn't baby it, but he keeps it meticulously clean. Dog hair does not bode well for his spotless interior.

Moments later, we're on the road, headed to Gravenhurst because our dog can't poop. What a wild Saturday.

We arrive at the animal hospital, which Zach called on the way, so we know we can go right inside. They're willing to take Bond in first thing as an emergency case just as a precaution. I make a mental note of that for the future, because not everyone would be so accommodating.

Like a typical male dog, Bond pees on the flower bed outside; one leg in the air as high as he can manage, and he hops along left to right as if he's trying to write his name in cursive. Once he's sufficiently marked that garden as his own, we walk inside to find a smiling receptionist. Bond is reluctant to walk through the door, but Isla coaxes him with a gentle voice, then rewards him with some ear scratches for a job well done.

Zach handles things with the receptionist, filling out the paperwork and giving our information, while Isla and I sit and wait on the opposite side of the room. Bond is shaking, leaning up against Isla for support. I now feel terrible for putting him through this. It's hard to explain to him that we're trying to keep him safe and healthy.

The veterinarian's assistant, Harriet, calls us in beyond the first door and asks us to have Bond step on the large scale. Bond weighs in at fifty pounds and Isla thinks that is another sign they are meant to be best friends, because she weighs the same. After Harriet records his weight, we enter an exam room and Zach lifts Bond up onto the table. Isla wants to sit with him, so like a good father, he lifts her up to sit beside her beloved pet.

Harriet, who has a bubbly personality and a New Zealand accent, does a quick check of Bond before announcing, "Dr. Russel will be in shortly. Just stay put and we'll have your fur baby taken care of in no time." She turns to walk through the door at the back of the room, opposite to where we entered.

I can tell Isla is feeling anxious—I am too—but I try to appear confident. Shoulders back, chin up, just like my momma always taught me.

Zach looks at me with a puzzled expression. "Are you trying to get the good doctor's services for free today?" he asks with a low voice, so Isla isn't able to hear.

"What? Why would you ask that?"

"You're standing here with your chest sticking out, and I have to admit, it's a bit distracting."

My face heats. I embarrass myself every time I leave the house. Ever since I started working from home, my already lacklustre social skills have become even worse. I decide to save myself further ridicule by sitting on a chair in the corner, crossing my arms over my chest and adding an exaggerated pout.

Zach laughs at my performance, but he's quickly distracted by the entrance of the veterinarian. A tall, robust man with light blond hair and grey eyes walks in wearing a navy polo shirt and khaki slacks with a stethoscope draped over his shoulders. I gather it's casual Saturday.

"Good morning. I'm Dr. Jack Russell." He reaches a hand out to shake with Zach.

I stay sitting in the corner, suppressing a laugh. Jack Russell? Jack Russell the vet? I wonder if that was a self-fulfilling prophecy. There's no way he doesn't see the comedic value there.

"What brings you in today, little fella?" Dr. Russell asks Bond.

Isla, who does not do well speaking to strangers at the best of times, doesn't miss a beat. "Well, this is my best friend, Bond. We only adopted him two days ago, but last night he ate the couch. Not the whole thing, you know. We don't know how much. But he sure ruined it. I don't think he meant to. He's the goodest boy in the whooooooole wide world. But he didn't want to eat his breakfast, and I made it just how he likes it. And he hasn't"—she leans in to whisper to the doctor—"gone doo-doo since yesterday." She places a hand over her mouth and giggles because at eight years old, poop talk is funny.

After Isla's excessively long explanation of what happened, Dr. Russell defers his questions to Zach, and they go back and forth in a question-answer conversation for a few moments.

Bond receives a thorough examination, and to my surprise he does really well. Isla had control of him like a Westminster dog handler. Dr. Russell declares he has no concerns, and doesn't think an x-ray is necessary, so we're just to monitor him for another twenty-four hours and if nothing changes, we come back.

Before we go, he reminds us to make sure we have enough safe chew toys available and to ensure he's getting a lot of exercise because a tired dog is less likely to get into trouble. I don't know how many more times a day my arm can handle throwing the ball for him—I feel like I'm going to need Tommy John surgery soon. And the lovely people at *Mullin's Pet Market* can attest to the fact we purchased a sufficient number of toys.

So, I guess we are on poop-watch until tomorrow. How did my life get so exciting?

We thank the doctor, and Zach lifts both Isla and Bond down from the counter. I don't feel any relief from the verdict we've gotten, but I guess the good thing is the vet isn't concerned.

Isla and I take Bond outside as Zach pays our bill. There isn't any area to let Bond run around, so we just walk him up and down the sidewalk a few hundred yards until Zach exits the building. We all pile in the SUV and head back home with no actual answers to the nagging question—why won't the dog poop?

Hours later, after we've had a pleasant lunch with Chelsea and Jasmine, the girls all rush off for Jasmine to show them the clothes she's brought for each of them. She makes such amazing creations, and it always brings a smile to Chelsea's face.

I'm standing outside with Bond again, waiting for his big moment; so far, no luck. He's running around, energetic as normal. We've played fetch for a while with no signs of discomfort or lethargy, so those are good signs, but he hasn't eaten or fertilized the yard.

"This is the last time I'm throwing it, then we have to go inside. It's getting cold." I don't think he understands what I'm saying. He's sitting in front of me, staring at the ball. I get the hint, so I throw the ball as far as I can—given my athletic skills, maybe twenty yards. I really should have Zach doing this because he was a college pitcher.

When Bond returns with the ball, I pick it up and place it on the patio table. "All done. We'll play again tomorrow." I turn to walk inside.

Bond sits on the deck, refusing to come inside, so I decide to try my hand at dog manipulation. "Fine, you don't want to come in? You'll have to stay out here while I eat the treats."

His one floppy ear perks up, but he still won't come inside. I close the door; each of us on opposite sides. I walk to the kitchen to get myself some water and find my handsome husband cleaning up the remaining lunch dishes. Once upon a time, I wouldn't have thought much of it, but right now, I don't think I could see a sexier sight. His dark jeans are low on his hips, and his charcoal grey T-shirt fits him perfectly. I'm sure I shrunk it in the wash, but I have no regrets.

"Are you just going to stare at me like I'm a piece of meat?" he jokes, interrupting my predatory stare.

"My apologies, Mr. Haynes. I was just admiring the view," I joke back without a hint of remorse. I walk up behind him, wrapping my arms around his torso. "Mr. Haynes, I detect the starting of a dad-bod under this T-shirt."

He spins around without breaking my grip and surprises me by lifting me onto the island countertop. "I am a dad, Mrs. Haynes. Do you have a problem with that?" He leans forward and meets me with a passionate kiss.

"Mr. Haynes. I do say. You are a phenomenal kisser." Before our interaction gains any more momentum, I hear scratching at the door, followed by a whine.

With one last brief kiss, Zach throws a tea towel over his shoulder and heads to the door to let the dog in. Bond runs in the house, zooming around as if someone turned his windup key. I laugh at his antics. He whips across the living room, paws skittering across the hardwood flooring, slides to a stop, lowers his front legs in a playful posture, then takes off running in the other direction. This continues for a few moments.

Once Isla returns downstairs, Bond runs to greet her. She squeals in delight as he licks her face. "Okay, okay. I missed you too." Her giggles fill the space with an echo on account of the missing furniture.

I realize if we're to host a baby shower here in two weeks, we're going to need some furniture. I disappear into my office so I can hunt online for some furniture. At this point, I'm not even picky about how it looks. It would be better to get something cheap in the event Bond destroys it again. I go to the local furniture store's website, sorting the results in ascending order of price. The first few options don't look very comfortable, so I decide on one which is slightly more expensive. I ask Zach's opinion and he gives the thumbs up to order the sofa and a new area rug. We'll see how long these last.

As long as I have everything for Quinn's baby shower, I'll be happy. Quinn was my rock for over a decade, always supporting and encouraging me. We met in our second year of university and quickly became best friends. We grew up only twenty minutes away from each other, but never met before then, with her in Bracebridge and me in Bala, on opposite sides of Lake Muskoka. I went to school in Gravenhurst while she attended a Catholic school in Bracebridge. Both of our husbands attended a secular high school in Bracebridge and played on the same baseball team. It's kind of funny how we all ended up in each other's lives so many years later.

My life wouldn't resemble anything it does now if it weren't for Quinn. This is the most important time in her life and if she asks me to rent an elephant, I will find a way. Okay, no I probably wouldn't because that's likely a source of animal cruelty, and as a vegetarian, I'm opposed to any sort of animal abuse, but I'd find a nice robotic, lifelike elephant.

After switching the light off in my office, it gets dark on account of the gloomy sky and falling outside. I step outside my office door and feel warmth squish between my toes.

I may be opposed to animal cruelty, but Bond does not oppose Zara cruelty.

At least we don't have to go back to the vet.

59

By Thursday evening, Bond has peed in each room of the house, despite his constant trips outside, and he's destroyed several hundred dollars worth of household items. I'm trying my best to be patient with him, but wow, it's been a challenge.

Isla is sleeping through the night, and that is a miracle. As a result, Chelsea has slept better, and therefore is less teenager-y. With them sleeping the past few nights, Zach and I have been able to spend uninterrupted time alone together; and well, it's just a win-win for everyone.

So, despite the obvious challenges Bond presents during this adjustment phase, he hasn't been without his benefits. I'm not sure Isla will ever choose to forge friendships with humans ever again, but we'll work on that down the road.

Chelsea is bringing her friend Liam over for us to meet him for the first time. I'm trying my best to be the cool mom and not embarrass the girl, but I took to the ferocious mother skill set naturally. He better not be some deadbeat kid that's taking advantage of Chelsea's naivety.

I'm trying to determine what to have for dinner when the door opens, and I hear two distinct voices enter. I wipe my hands on a kitchen towel and walk toward the sound. Next to Chelsea is a devastatingly handsome young man. He has beautiful golden skin, stunning hazel eyes with gold flecks sparkling under our overhead lighting, and black hair styled neatly in a fade with a little curly length on top.

What makes him genuinely attractive is how he speaks to me.

"Hello, Mrs. Haynes. You have a beautiful home. Thank you for having me." He reaches out to shake my hand.

I stop myself from pulling him into a hug and thanking him for being Chelsea's friend, because that would mortify the poor girl. "Thank you, Liam. It's nice to meet you. Come on in and make yourself at home. If you need anything, just ask."

"Thank you, Ma'am."

I cringe at the term 'Ma'am.' "Oh, Zara will be fine, Liam. You don't need to be formal. I'm not even that much older than you."

Both Liam and Chelsea laugh. Full belly laughs.

I stand there staring at them, waiting for them to let me in on the joke with my head tilted and my eyebrows threatening to touch in the centre of my face.

When they stop laughing a few seconds later—which really felt excessive—Chelsea clears her throat as she catches my gaze. "Sorry, Zara. That was just funny." They both start chuckling again.

Teenagers. I'm thirty years old; I'm not a dinosaur.

As I shoo them away, I tell them they can go upstairs as long as they leave the door open. I'll bribe Isla with ice cream to walk past every few minutes and check on them. She'll make a great snitch.

I was the youngest of three girls by a significant margin, so I am well versed in spying-for-mom side jobs. I scored a lot of Oreos by agreeing to tattle on my sisters if there was ever the need. By the time I hit the troublesome teen years, I'd seen my sisters do just about everything and it scared me out of ever misbehaving.

Now they're both married with kids of their own. Noa has twins who are close to Chelsea's age, Caleb and Sophie, and Lexi has a girl and two boys, Hollis, Oscar, and Ethan. We don't see each other a lot because of busy schedules, and the fact we were never close to begin with, but I love my sisters and their kids. Their husbands—I could take them or leave them.

After twenty minutes, Isla tiptoes her way downstairs, looking like she has some juicy gossip to share. I brace myself for hearing Chelsea and Liam are making out in her room or some other awkward scenario.

Isla giggles, and my entire body tenses—the exact opposite of how I normally respond to her sweet sound. "They're doing homework."

I shake my head, wondering if I've misheard her. "Excuse me. What? Homework?" I'm staring down at this small human with her loyal companion at her side. "Did they pay you to tell me that?"

She twists her face in a way that would be comical if I wasn't trying to grill her right now, but I have to keep my serious mom face on. "No, they're really doing homework. I like Liam. He makes me laugh."

Wow. She went and spoke to him? And he left a good impression? Maybe I need to loosen the reins on Chelsea a little and allow her to make decisions without my input.

Zach walks in the side door from the garage, and Bond is quick to greet him. Isla is nearly as fast but has to wait for Bond to finish his welcome-home ritual. His tail whirls around with a velocity that makes it nearly disappear.

I'm third in line in the welcome-home brigade, reaching up on my tiptoes to plant a kiss on my husband. He looks like he's had a long day, with his lips in a tight, forced smile and his green eyes framed by dark circles underneath.

"Hey, are you all right?" I question him, biting my lower lip.

"Just a long day. I had to fire Candi." He runs his hand through his messy hair.

I suppress a smile. Firing an employee shouldn't make me happy because finding and training a new receptionist isn't a simple task, but Candi tried to cause trouble for Zach and me before we were married and has been a thorn in my side ever since. I can't say I'm sad to see her go, but for Zach's sake, I'll try to be sympathetic.

"What happened?"

He strides over to take a seat on our new couch—which is far less comfortable than our old sofa—throws his feet up and lies back to melt some of the tension of the day away. "I didn't want to say anything because I didn't want you worrying about it. You're the only woman for me and I'd never cheat on you. Ever. You know that, right?"

I feel a lump form in my throat that I can't swallow, so I nod.

"Candi has been getting more and more brazen the past few weeks with her flirting and touching."

Touching? Oh. No. She. Didn't.

"So many times, I told her to stop, but she just couldn't take no for an answer. Today, she took it a step too far, and I couldn't take it anymore. I told her to clean out her desk and leave."

I breathe a sigh of relief knowing she's out of our lives—for good—but my relief quickly morphs to anger. A wash of fury comes over me that's so intense, I can feel my core temperature rise. I'm furious that Zach had to put up with persistent sexual harassment and still tried to give her the benefit of the doubt because, otherwise, she was a decent employee. If roles were reversed, he'd probably be facing criminal charges right now.

I drop next to Zach, lying parallel with him so I can snuggle into his chest. "I'm so sorry, Honey. You shouldn't have had to deal with that. I can't believe her! I'm not the violent type, but if I see her at the grocery store, best believe there will be a cat fight in the produce section."

Zach lets out a low chuckle, smirking at me. He thinks I'm kidding. Cute.

"I would like front-row seats to that show."

I arch my neck up to plant a kiss on him, knowing Isla and Bond have disappeared into the backyard. We take advantage of the alone time and get lost in each other for a moment.

Then I hear a throat clearing. I freeze for a brief second before I lift my head to see Liam and a horrified Chelsea standing at the bottom of the stairs. Part of me wants to stand up, puff out my chest, and say, "Yeah! I'm young. I've still got it!" It's really is tempting after our earlier encounter by I reel in my crazy so I don't embarrass Chelsea any more.

"Hey, Chels. Liam. Uh. What are you guys up to?"

"Well, we were coming down to grab something to eat, but I'm not really hungry now."

My cheeks flush as I hop off the couch.

Zach follows suit. He redirects the conversation after glancing at the awkward faces we're all sporting. "You must be Liam. I'm Zach, Chelsea's... uh... I don't know what she calls me."

"Zach. I just call you Zach. Sometimes I call you the first man I ever trusted, but that's less often." Chelsea's mouth drops open a touch before her eyes dart to the floor.

I gather she didn't mean to blurt that out. Hearing those words both warms and pains my heart.

Liam reaches his hand out to shake Zach's. "Nice to meet you, Sir. Thank you for having me."

"Oh, you don't have to call me Sir. Zach is fine. I'm really not that old."

This time, I join in on the laughter with Liam and Chelsea. Zach, at thirty-two, is the oldest person in the house, and even if he's still young, to teenagers, he's old. He missed the joke.

Isla and Bond choose that exact moment to come back inside. Bond runs over to Liam, dancing around him like he does with Zach. In all honesty, it's always the dog's opinion that is the most trustworthy. Liam is a keeper.

We sit together as a family for dinner, Liam included. He is such a natural addition to our little unit, I keep forgetting today is the first time we've met. He's a nice young man. Polite, respectful, helpful, and kind. He is also funny once he gets comfortable and I notice Chelsea laugh a handful of times.

I may not be a huge fan of a relationship for her right now, as she's still struggling with a lot of adjustments and past issues, but I have to admit, she could do worse. She keeps insisting they are just friends, but I can see the way Liam looks at her, and I'm not sure they will stay that way.

We learn that his mother is a doctor at the local hospital and came from Nigeria as a child. Liam's father is of Irish heritage, but it was his great-grandfather who immigrated to Canada over 100 years ago. His father works as an accountant out of their home just five minutes away.

As an only child, it granted Liam every opportunity to pursue sports, arts, and academics. Those opportunities have molded him into a focused young man with the goal of pursuing business with his post-secondary education, though he hasn't narrowed down which aspect of business yet. He still has another twenty months of high school, so he's got plenty of time to decide.

All in all, the entire family warms to him, and even Isla, who struggles in social settings with unfamiliar people, embraced him without hesitation. I have a suspicion we'll be seeing a lot more of Liam.

"So, Liam." My words draw his attention, but he doesn't look the slightest bit nervous. "Chelsea mentioned you offered to pick her up or drive her home from school. Is that something you're still interested in, Chels?"

"I am if you're okay with it." Her eyes dart from Zach to me.

"I've got no problem with that," Zach clarifies.

"I think it will be okay, too. But if you're ever going anywhere else other than straight home, let me know, okay?" I make it clear I need to always be informed of her whereabouts.

"Yeah, I can do that. I don't have anywhere exciting to be, anyway. It just makes sense, since he was offering. It will save you guys from having to pick me up and drop me off." She's nonchalant about the whole scenario. She's being too cool right now.

Perhaps I have misread the situation, and they are just friends. My instincts are not as refined as I wish they were. I sit in my seat, contemplating all I know about life, getting lost down the rabbit-hole of what else I may have been wrong about in my thirty years on Earth.

Zach interrupts my thoughts when he stands up and collects the dishes from in front of everyone at our long rectangular dining table. I take a moment to be grateful the dog hasn't eaten it—or peed on it.

Liam stands and helps Zach with the dishes. I want to protest, because he's our guest, but I'm secretly hoping Zach will have a "guy talk" with Liam in the kitchen and get some more insight into the situation. Bond follows the haul of dirty dishes into the kitchen, probably hoping he's on dish-duty tonight.

The girls and I stay at the table, where I make fleeting eye contact with Chelsea before she turns her gaze in another direction. I wish for a split second I had mind-reading abilities, but quickly change my mind because in my years of being a counsellor, and from my experience—not that long ago, thank you very much—the teenage brain is often a mess of emotions and uncertainties. Perhaps a direct approach is best.

"So, Chels. Liam's pretty hunky." I wink. Not creepy at all.

My cougar-esque comment disturbs Chelsea as much as it did me.

"All the girls at school seem to think so."

Unhelpful.

"Does he have a girlfriend? Or a special someone?"

She glares at me for a moment, and I realize we've gotten our wires crossed.

"Oh gosh, Chels. Sorry. I was trying to figure out if *you* like him!"

A look of relief sweeps across her face. "Oh, I was worried you…"

Nope. Big nope. That sentence does not need to be finished. Why am I so hopeless? I interrupt Chelsea before she can say another word. "No! Good grief, Chels. I'm a happily married woman."

"Yeah. She says Daddy is a dreamboat," Isla adds in, helpfully.

"Exactly. The dreamiest dreamboat to ever set sail on the sea of love."

I'm pretty sure Chelsea suppresses a gag at my admission, but she witnessed me boarding the dreamboat earlier. She can't be the least bit surprised.

"Right. Anyway, no. I don't like him like that. He's nice, and he is a good friend, but he's more like a brother."

Well, that's settled then. Looking at Chelsea's face, I don't detect a hint of dishonesty in her words. I surmise they are just friends. Now I can rest easy, not having to stress about 'the sex talk' just yet. Talking to Isla about puberty has me stressing enough—with her being homeschooled, I can't hand off responsibility to anyone else to cover these awkward topics.

Zach and Liam re-enter the dining room carrying a pint of ice cream, strawberries, bowls, and spoons. Isla's face looks elated as she licks her lips. She's practically panting like a dog, making me realize our dog is absent.

"Where's Bond?" I ask Zach.

His eyes dart to Liam, whose eyes widen. A second later, they are both laughing.

Zach finally responds, "He's uh… earning his keep."

"Please tell me the dog is not in there licking all the dishes." I smirk, but I can hear the plates being pushed around the tile floor.

"Okay. I won't tell you." He smiles and opens the ice cream container. "Who wants dessert?"

His question is met with cheers from Isla, so he scoops out spheres of pink ice cream, placing a few fresh strawberries on top. We chatter about random things while we eat our sweet treat, and the evening passes too quickly.

A short while later, Liam announces he should get home, but he'll be back in the morning to pick up Chelsea for school.

I let Bond outside after he's done his chores, finish cleaning up from dinner, then read a book to Isla called *Marvellous Macey, The Delightful Days*. The story has Isla giggling, smiling and asking a *lot* of questions. I tuck her in as Bond curls up on the dog bed beside her. He does this for show, because the moment I step out of the room, he'll be taking over Isla's bed.

I stand at the bedroom door for a moment watching this sweet girl and her best friend in the glow of her night light. Tears spring from my eyes when I think about how just two weeks ago she'd have so much anxiety over going to bed, because she never knew what her night terrors would torment her with. I'm so relieved she can finally get some much-needed rest.

Zach comes up the stairs and catches me leaning on the doorframe. He snakes his arms around me from behind, pulling me into his chest and resting his chin on the top of my head.

"What are you doing, Baby?"

"Just watching her. It's hard to imagine this little ray of sunshine has seen so much darkness," I whisper.

"I know. We can't protect them from everything; especially the past."

He's right. I know he's right; but I'll spend every waking moment trying.

The day of Quinn's baby shower arrives, and I'd like to say I'm running around like a chicken with my head cut off, but I'm not nearly *that* coordinated. For a type-A personality, I'm surprisingly disorganized. I have Zach hanging decorations. The girls are arranging the few games we have set up. I'm spinning around in circles, wondering what to do next.

I had no clue that planning a baby shower was so much work, or I may have suggested just renting a banquet hall. To make things easier, I hired the same caterers we used for our wedding only a few months ago and contacted my friend Desirea from *Desirea's Sweets* to provide a cake. She made the cakes for both mine and Quinn's weddings, so she's overjoyed when I tell her Quinn is expecting. She creates a sugary, three-tiered masterpiece that's surely to provide me with breakfast for the next few days. Really, it's a raspberry and lemon cake, so it's practically a muffin.

While the caterers finish getting the food set up, I run upstairs to shower and change. I've been stress-cleaning and decorating all morning and need to freshen up before guests arrive.

My dress is a cobalt blue vintage swing dress, which is presentable, but comfortable enough to perform my hosting duties. I figured since I'm guessing Quinn is having a boy, blue was the obvious choice.

Zach is also on "Team Boy," but I think it may only be because he refuses to wear pink.

My mother Alanna, sisters Noa and Lexi, and their kids are the first to arrive. I greet everyone with a hug, rustling little Oscar's hair and picking him up for a thorough squeeze. I missed my little snuggle buddy. My family all came early to ask if I needed any help. Thankfully, everything is set up and ready, so I have a few minutes to visit with them before the chaos starts.

Chelsea disappears with Caleb and Sophie, while Isla takes off with Lexi's three kids and Bond. The festivities will probably bore them, so I told them they can entertain themselves elsewhere.

Moments later, the guests of honour arrive. Tyler parks their black SUV and hops out to run around and open Quinn's door. When she exits the vehicle, she looks more beautiful than ever in a dusty mauve, knee-length wrap dress that hugs her rounded stomach. She styled her blonde hair in beachy waves that look effortless, but probably took some time to achieve. Her skin is glowing and her blue eyes radiate happiness. Tyler leads Quinn by the hand up the few steps to our front door. I open it without waiting for them to knock.

Quinn squeals with delight as she wraps me in a hug. We used to see each other often, but now, with life getting in the way, those visits are getting less frequent. Zach and Tyler do the typical "bro" greeting with the handshake-slash-hug-slash-back-slap move. I love seeing the two of them together because they light up each other's eyes in ways a wife just can't. Like I need my Quinn time, Zach and Tyler need their bro time.

I lead the couple into the house, showing them the décor and explaining the plan for the day. I'll blame Quinn's reaction on pregnancy emotions because she's never been one to cry over streamers and balloons before.

Once she's wiped the tears from her eyes, the first thing she asks is, "Did you get a new couch?"

I forgot to tell her about our adventure with the couch foam, so I quickly fill her in. Tears of laughter replace her previous tears. She stops herself from laughing by announcing, "Don't make me laugh. I'm going to pee myself."

"Well, that's a situation only you can control, Amiga."

My sisters and mom all chime in about their leaky, post-pregnancy bladders and bond over the dangers of sneezing. It seems like a silly thing to be sad about, but it upsets me every once in a while that I can never carry children of my own. I hate that I'll never know what a child would look like with the perfect mix of my features and Zach's. I'll never know how it feels for the man I love to touch my belly in anticipation of fluttering kicks. I'll never even know what it's like to fear a sneezing fit after drinking a latte.

As I travel down the path of depressing thoughts, Zach interrupts me. "Are you okay, Baby? What can I help with?" He's come up behind me, wrapping his arms around me in a tight squeeze, placing his chin on my shoulder.

I nod and try to smile at him, but his angle makes it difficult. His interruption is welcome because it stopped my pervading thoughts. Before I can speak, I take a breath to compose myself. "I'm fine." I spin around in his grip, stand on my tippy toes to give him a peck on the cheek, which elicits a smile. "Everything is under control."

He leans in to kiss my forehead as more guests arrive. Some teachers Quinn works with, a few old college friends, and members of her and Tyler's families have filled the main floor of our home to capacity. The gift table is overflowing, and it shows me that Quinn, Tyler, and the unknown baby are loved dearly.

Chatter is buzzing, the temperature is rising on account of the caterers preparing food and the body heat being created, and I'm overwhelmed by the crowd that has formed in my home. The younger kids have come back downstairs, along with the dog, and they're running around, weaving in between adults who are all performing juggling acts with appetizers and drinks. Foresight tells me I'm going to need another new area rug in the near future.

I stand with my back to the wall, scanning the room, having to remind myself to breathe. I will not ruin Quinn's day by having a panic attack.

Breathe in… two… three. Breathe out… two… three.

This time, Quinn is the one to notice the change in my demeanour and strides… err… waddles over with a concerned look on her face. "What's wrong, Chica?" She places a gentle hand on my left forearm and stands in front of me, staying focused on my eyes. She is an expert in Zara-panic-attacks after more than eleven years of friendship.

"I'm fine." I repeat for the second time in a short period, even though I'm not feeling fine at all. "Just taking a breather. It's hot in here. Maybe I should go open my office window to let a little air in." I turn to go do just that, but Quinn's dainty hand stops me with a firm grip.

"Please, tell me if something is wrong. I don't want to stress you out."

"You're not!" I say, a little too eagerly. "I mean, it's not you at all. You know how I am with crowds. I just need a minute."

"Well, let's go take a minute in your office then." She grabs my hand and walks me to my office, opening the door and waddling inside. I note how her motherly instincts are already getting practice, leading her thirty-year-old best friend out of a crowd to be coddled.

I walk over to open the window behind my desk, tucking away the few papers left out so they won't blow around in the breeze. The cool air helps to calm me as I breathe in the crisp air. My body temperature comes down and my heart rate decreases. Crisis averted.

"Has everything been okay lately? I've been a crap friend ever since I got married and I haven't been checking on you."

"Quinn, you have your own life and responsibilities. I don't want to be a burden you have to 'check on' all the time."

"Nope." She looks at me with a fierce determination that gives me goosebumps.

Tentatively, I ask, "Nope, what?"

"Nope, you are not starting this whole 'I'm a burden' stuff again, because you *have* never been, nor *will* ever be, a burden. I'm asking because I want to know. I want to be here for you like you always are for me."

As much as I try, I don't feel like I'm always here for Quinn. It's more often the other way around. Battling generalized anxiety disorder along with depression and a panic disorder, sometimes being in my head is too much to manage and I disappear from everyone's radar. The past few months since being married and essentially forming an insta-family, even though my mental health has been stable with the use of medication and therapy, I have been so busy in my own world, I haven't been a great friend. I know arguing with her is a waste of what little energy I have, though, so I don't resort to self-deprecating comments.

"You are always there when I need you, Quinny. Everything is fine."

"Fine. Fine. You always say everything is fine. Your face says otherwise, Zara." She lets out a frustrated exhale before taking a seat on the beige linen sofa I reserve for my patients. "Just talk to me. You've taken on a lot this year, and you know how beneficial a set of listening ears can be."

I can't argue there. My career is based on that fact.

"I'm just a little overwhelmed. It's not that anyone else is too much or causing any issues. The girls are great, and Zach is like, from another world because he's so amazing."

Quinn makes an exaggerated gagging sound, which makes me giggle. She's equally obsessed with Tyler.

"It's just hard because I constantly feel like I'm doing everything wrong, or not good enough to care for these amazing people. I struggle to feel worthy of having the potential to be so happy."

Seconds pass that feel like minutes. I'm clawing at the skin on my arms underneath my blouse.

Finally, Quinn speaks. "I'm not a mom yet, so I can't say for sure, but I'd be willing to bet that those two girls of yours are not keeping track of the ways you've failed them. They're both happy, healthy, and loved. Being a parent—being responsible for another human being—it's a tough gig, and you took it on without hesitation. Your love for them is what matters, and you have that in spades."

Tyler interrupts our little girl chat by peeking his head in the door. "There's my beautiful baby-momma. You're being requested by our child's grandmothers."

Quinn looks to me for approval, so without acknowledging her words, I say, "Let's get you back to your party."

I return to the chaos, grateful for the moment I had to breathe.

Of all the things I expected to see when I returned to the living room, Isla's giggling surprises me as she shouts, "Look, Mommy! Bond is trying to push Oscar like a baby stroller!"

I glance up to see Bond with his paws on Oscar's shoulders, frantically trying to show Oscar who the big dog is around here. When the adults in the room burst out laughing and Bond runs outside, I relax my horrified expression.

Lexi isn't traumatized, based on the tears of laughter running down her face. Little Oscar skips off, oblivious to the fact Bond was being a dog—not getting into the theme of the baby shower.

"That was an interesting turn of events," Quinn quips. Tyler is trying to compose himself, as are all the other adults in the room. I'm not sure if they're laughing about the episode, or Isla's interpretation of what happened.

Judging by the temperature of my cheeks, my face must border on scarlet. I'm mortified, but everyone seems to have taken it in good humour. Leave it to the dog to turn an innocent co-ed baby shower X-rated.

I walk through our main floor to peek out the back window and see the four younger kids standing on the deck, taking turns throwing the ball out into the yard for Bond to fetch. Hopefully they can tire him out so he'll behave himself for the rest of the afternoon. I'm hopeful, but realistic. There has yet to be one day which Bond has behaved himself from dawn until dusk.

The caterers are flitting around the house, doing their well-rehearsed dance around guests with trays, placing food out for people to munch on as they mingle. They've prepared an array of different items from Vietnamese spring rolls to bruschetta to cheese fondue. Desirea created a beautiful cake with white buttercream icing piped to perfection. The masterpiece is the focal point of the food table, and I, for one, can't wait to dig in. We also have some chocolate truffles and miniature cheesecakes with various toppings—including Oreo, of course.

I ask Zach to call the kids in from outside so they can come get something to eat. I announce to everyone that the next round of food is ready, and people pile into the dining room area, where everything is set up on our large table. The buffet style set-up works well as everyone works their way around the table. That is, until Hollis drops her plate on the floor by accident.

Before I can even think about cleaning it up, Bond is on the scene. He slurps up a deviled egg, a spring roll, some raw vegetables and the fondue covered bread with no consideration for how much that cost per serving. He didn't even taste any of it. I'm grateful, however, that I don't have to find suitable cleaning supplies to clean up a mess that included both solids and liquids.

As I walk over to comfort Hollis, who has tears glistening in her eyes, Isla praises Bond for a job well done. Bond seems to misunderstand the praise and takes it as an invitation to clean up some more—from the table. His front paws pop up, landing next to the tray of deviled eggs, and he grabs a mouthful so fast I don't have time to react.

"Bond!" I shout, which draws the attention of anyone else who wasn't already watching. "Bad dog! No!"

The furry bandit sits beside the table, tongue flicking around, probably trying to clear the residual egg yolks from the roof of his mouth, and acts like the world's best dog. He really doesn't see the issue with helping himself from the table, but after Zach's habit of letting Bond help with dish duty, I can't really blame him. Still, it's not behaviour I want to encourage.

Isla puts down her own plate she has only a quarter filled, and calls Bond toward the back door again. She crouches down beside him as he sits, listening to her attentively. I can barely hear her speak over the chaos in the house, but it is something along the lines of being a good boy, so he won't have to go live somewhere else. I see the emotion pour from her eyes, and it hurts my heart to see her so concerned.

I weave my way through the bodies crowded around the dining table so I can speak to Isla. "Sweetheart, please don't worry. We're not going to get rid of Bond just because he doesn't know the rules yet. He's still a kid, and he's just learning."

She looks up at me with her mouth dropped open and her eyebrows raised over her wide, ocean-blue eyes. "Really? You're not going to make him leave?"

I'm confused why she's so concerned about him being sent away for eating food—especially since I've been the victim of multiple dog-poop pedicure treatments. Stealing food isn't going to be the tipping point. I don't want to press the issue, so

I just reassure her Bond is safe here, and we will not make him find another home.

She relaxes enough that she walks back to pick up her abandoned plate and continues to grab a few extra items from the table. Given how much she eats on a normal day, I suspect that those extra items are for her best friend—the shaggy swindler trailing behind her.

After we've eaten, we take a break from scarfing down calories in excess to partake in a few games I've come up with—well, that I found on Pinterest and thought I could pull off.

Tyler and Quinn both laugh, smile, and cry through the games and gift opening. They will cherish the sentimental items their baby received for years to come and each one shows how anticipated his or her arrival into the world is. Zach and I purchased the car-seat and stroller set Quinn requested on her registry, but we've kept that hidden for now.

As she reaches to open the decoy gift I got for her, I feel anxiety rising in my stomach. I wasn't aware that it was a 'thing' for people to read the entire card out loud at baby showers.

She takes the card from the top of the package and slides her delicate finger under the seal, pulling the card out to read aloud. "Quinn, I struggle to put into words exactly how much you mean to me. You came into my life when I felt like nothing could permeate the darkness I was surrounded by. Like a never-ceasing ray of sunshine, you lit my way back to life..." She's crying so hard by the time she finishes the first few sentences, she passes the card to Tyler, and he doesn't miss the implied instruction.

"Without you, I wouldn't have survived, and that's not an exaggeration. I don't have to question whether or not you'll be a wonderful mother, because I know from experience, when you love, you love with your whole heart. Your child is beyond lucky to have you by their side from their first breath onward." Tyler looks up through his moist eyes, directly at me. "I agree with you there." He places an arm around Quinn as he continues, "Being able to watch you raise a human will be one of the greatest honours of my life. As the day you will welcome the third member of your family draws closer, I find myself overcome by my own love for the beautiful bundle you'll soon hold in your arms. As we enter this next chapter of our lives together, I couldn't ask for a better friend to have new milestones, adventures, and firsts alongside. Your forever best friend, Zara."

A crying Quinn comes shuffling toward me and throws me in a python-grip hug I've become accustomed to. The difference this time, I feel a lofty kick right in my abdomen as Quinn presses against me. She pulls back and rubs her hand on her belly. "They say thank you too, Auntie Zara."

Like the awkward person I am, I lean down to address my future niece or nephew. "I love you so much, little one." My admission only causes more tears to flow from Quinn. She's never been a crier before, so I think there really is something to this pregnancy hormone stuff. Something else I'll never get to experience firsthand.

I stand back up to come face to face with Quinn—well, eye to lips because she's three inches taller than I am—and say, "Go open your gift now, Mommy."

Her eyes light up at the term "mommy" and she rubs her perfectly round belly again. She toddles back to her seat, and Tyler places the large box on the chair he vacated. Quinn peels back the metallic silver wrapping paper, with a patience I certainly wouldn't have, and seems to enjoy every moment of the process. Once the box is exposed, she shoots me a confused look. I wrapped the gifts together in a toaster oven box. I knew it would leave her scratching her head.

She tears open the top, now losing all signs of patience, and starts pulling out the items one by one. I went on an Etsy binge shopping spree, buying items for expectant mothers that have all been custom made. Quinn pulls out the soft cotton robe, hospital gown, slippers and sleep mask in the first package. The crowd gathered around does their obligatory "oooh, ahhh." The next package includes lotions, potions, and whatever perineal spray is. Sounds like the kind of thing I'm glad I don't know about. I also purchased her a necklace with a sweet poem in the box, a T-shirt that says "Ice, Ice" across the chest with an arrow pointing downward, a pair of socks that say "Baby, coming soon" so she can wear them during labour, and a few other goodies.

Right on time, Zach reappears from the laundry room, where we had the stroller hidden, to parade their actual gift through the house. I didn't think it through, because it causes me far more emotional distress to see Zach pushing a baby stroller than I ever would have expected.

My expression betrays how I am feeling, even though I try my best to maintain my smiling face. This time, it's my mom who notices, and I'm thinking I have a marquis ticker across my forehead that displays whenever I'm having 'a moment.' Like red flashing letters blink left to right, "Zara is on the verge of a breakdown. Proceed with caution."

"Are you okay, my darling?"

"Of course. I'm totally fine. Everything is fine."

Once everyone leaves, including the caterers who cleaned up ninety percent of the mess, and the kids are in bed, I collapse onto the couch. Zach comes and sits at the opposite end, lifting my feet so he can slide in underneath them. He rubs my tired feet, and I silently wish to myself these little tender touches never disappear as our years of marriage tick on.

"Are you okay, Baby?"

I've been asked that a lot today. I give him a simple, "Mm-hmm." I don't really want to bring up events that happened in the past that I thought I had accepted. After having a hysterectomy at the ripe old age of eighteen because of trauma, I struggled to move beyond it for a long time.

"Are you sure?"

I close my eyes and release a sigh, trying to focus on his touch, and what I should say in response—if I should say anything. I talk myself into telling him what's on my mind because I have learned honesty is the best policy, even when it's uncomfortable. "I just…" I take another deep breath to steady my voice. I do not want to cry. "I had a hard time being reminded that it will never be us welcoming a baby. You'll never push our baby in a stroller or feel our baby kick in my belly. We'll never get to do that. And of course I love our girls, and wouldn't change a thing, but it was hard to be reminded all day that we'll never get those experiences."

Zach takes a moment before responding, and lifts my feet to escape under them, only to lay his muscular body on top of mine, using his forearms to support himself so I'm not crushed. "The things I heard today about labour and childbirth, I'm glad you never have to go through it."

That wasn't the response I expected, so I probe him for more. "What do you mean?"

"Well, people talk about the 'magic' of childbirth, sure, but when I heard your mom and sisters talking today, I was kind of horrified. Did you know that a lot of women poop during labour? Or vomit? Not to mention everyone in the room seeing your downstairs! I don't mean to sound like a dictator, but I'd like to keep some things for myself." He draws a circle in the air around my um… downstairs, as he so eloquently put it.

I can't help but laugh. "I know labour isn't glamorous, but I still get sad sometimes when I realize we'll never get to experience it."

"We'll never get to experience the crying baby up all night, no sex for weeks, leaky bladder, diapers, pureed carrots, teething, and all the other hard parts of raising a baby either. We created our family unconventionally, but I have no regrets. I love you, Zara Rihanna Haynes. I love you so much, and I wouldn't change a thing about the life we have together." He reaches up to wipe the tear off of my cheek before planting a kiss on me that makes me forget about all the thoughts rolling through my head. He has a knack for bringing me back to the present and stopping my unrelenting worrying about the what-ifs and what-could-have-beens.

"I love you," I whisper once we break apart.

Zach's smile makes happiness and contentment wash over me. He grabs my hands, raising me to my feet, then throws me over his shoulder in a fireman's carry. I squirm and squeal for him to put me down, but he just laughs and walks up the stairs, carrying me as if I weigh nothing.

"Where are you taking me?"

"To bed." He speaks with such confidence, he leaves no room for questions.

I wake up feeling a line of sunshine across my face. I turn to my left to greet Zach, only to find he's not here. It doesn't happen often, as we usually wake up at the same time, and I have to admit, I hate waking up to an empty bed.

Faint giggling and dog claws skittering across the floor float up from downstairs, so I guess everyone is up. When I pick up my phone to glance at the time, I realize it's ten o'clock. Sleeping in so late indicates how much socializing exhausts me.

After brushing my teeth, washing my face, and making myself presentable, I walk downstairs to find the kitchen looking like a flour bomb went off. My heart rate speeds up, but I take a second to remind myself it's just a little mess. It's not a big deal.

"Oh, uh... Good morning, Baby. Isla and I were just making pancakes."

I slowly make my way into the kitchen, surveying the damage. There is flour spread in a fine dust from floor to ceiling. "What happened?" I ask as my eyes continue to scan the area.

"Well, um... Isla was grabbing the flour from the pantry and..."

At that moment, Bond runs across the floor looking more like a Samoyed than a German shepherd and Chelsea enters the room from the stairs behind me. "Wow! What happened in here?"

The look on my face doesn't escape Zach's notice. "Sorry. Bond ran in front of her as she was walking, and she tripped with the bag of flour." He rattles his words out fast enough, I barely register what he's said.

Isla is trying to control her giggles, albeit unsuccessfully. I have even less success, as I burst out laughing. Everyone else takes a second to see if it's because I find the situation funny or if I'm on the verge of a total breakdown. Either or is possible, but right now, I'm focusing on the humour. You either laugh or cry in these situations.

Without thinking, I reach my hand into the bag of flour, grab a handful and whip it at Zach, coating his left cheek in white powder. He sputters his lips to spit out what got into his mouth and for a moment, I feel terrible. My regret is short-lived when he picks up his own handful and throws it back at me. Before long, the entire family—all five of us—are caked in flour. The house is a disaster, and it's the most fun we've had in recent memory.

Once the fun is over, we spend the next four solid hours cleaning flour from every nook and cranny in our kitchen and ourselves. To keep the fun alive, we have music blaring through the house, and we're dancing, singing, and having wooden-spoon karaoke battles. Flour isn't easy to clean up, we've learned, so it takes several passes with our sponges and rags before we rid the surfaces of the hazy film it leaves behind.

We give Bond a bath, which proves to be a challenge. They gave him a bath at Carter's, so I know this isn't his first time, but he sure gave us a workout. We had to hose him off outside in a preliminary rinse, so we didn't end up clogging the drains with flour paste and hair. I suspect I will find a poop pile strategically placed as a booby trap to express his displeasure. He's no longer speaking to me.

Chelsea asks if Liam can come over after we've gotten everything cleaned up. They have some schoolwork to get done before tomorrow, so I'm not about to stand in the way of academic progress.

When Liam arrives, he knocks on the door and Chelsea comes skidding across the floor from nowhere shouting, "I'll get it!" She races to the door and breathlessly answers, "Hey, Liam. Come on in."

I'm baffled by the encounter because I thought we settled that she didn't have a crush on him, but her eagerness to be the one to greet him says otherwise. Teenagers.

"Hi, Liam," I holler from the living room sofa. I've just sat down to watch repeats of an old TV show I'm planning to absorb myself in it until dinnertime. Maybe I'll even order pizza so I can keep watching.

"Hi, Ma—"

"Zara!" I interrupt. "No ma'am business here, Liam. Zara. Just Zara."

"Right. Sorry, Zara. My parents taught me to respect my elders, so it's a habit."

Elders. I was in grade eight when this guy was born. He acts like I'm an octogenarian. "It's a wonderful habit, and your parents have raised a wonderful young man, but please don't make me feel old."

Now I've made the kid feel bad because he hangs his head and stares at the floor. Why am I such a screwup? People think I am angry at them for being respectful. I am such a jerk.

"I'm sorry, Liam. I appreciate your manners. There is no need to be formal; I want you to feel comfortable here."

Liam lifts his head to meet my eyes and gives me a nod in acknowledgement but doesn't speak.

"Help yourselves to whatever you want in the kitchen. I'm going to binge watch my show for a while." If I scare away Chelsea's one friend, I will never forgive myself.

The kids wander off; I sink back onto the couch, throw my feet up, and just about hit play when I hear Zach yell, "Zara? A little help here?"

I walk upstairs to find Zach standing in our bedroom in a flurry of feathers. It appears our down-filled pillows did not survive Bond's wrath. This must be his way of telling us off for his hose down in the yard.

Zach is standing by our bathroom door, wearing only a towel. Judging by his reaction, I'd say Bond murdered the pillows in the few minutes it took Zach to shower.

I reach over to flick off the ceiling fan so our room will look less like a snow globe. Once the feathers settle, they stick to every surface with the slightest static charge. I don't think a broom is going to tackle this.

"I'll go get the Shop Vac from the garage." Zach pulls on a pair of boxers and removes his towel to dry his hair. Once again, he catches me leering at him. "My eyes are up here, baby." He laughs.

"I don't want to look at your eyes, *Baby.*"

"What *do* you want to look at?" he asks, striding across the room, swiftly grabbing me, then pulling me onto his lap as he sits on the end of the bed. Even if I had time to protest, I wouldn't have. "These feathers are poking my butt," he declares, disrupting any romance in the works.

"Wow, what happened in here now?" Chelsea's voice chimes in from the doorway. Once she peeks her head inside and sees me seated on Zach's lap, she backs out and says something to Liam. They must have been coming to ask something and now we've scared them off with our PDA— private display of affection.

Zach and I both laugh at how easy it is to send her scrambling. She wasn't around a lot of affection growing up, so it's foreign to her. Plus, we're her parents, so I think that's traumatic for any teenager.

Since butt feathers and teen interruptions squashed our potential for romance, I hop off Zach's lap. "I'll go get garbage bags."

I feel like we should perform the team huddle ritual. "Ready? Break!" But I don't suggest it. We each complete our agreed upon tasks and arrive back in our bedroom to tackle the pillow slaughter.

Our grand total for the day amounts to six hours of cleaning up Bond-caused messes, and after the socializing and activity of yesterday, I am totally exhausted.

I decide pizza is the best choice for dinner, and being the sweet young man he is, Liam offers to go pick it up. He and Chelsea drive into town and return home thirty minutes later with dinner. We sit down for another enjoyable family meal, with Liam feeling every bit as part of the family as the rest of us. He seamlessly fits into our dynamic, and aside from the fact he thinks I'm old, he's a pleasure to have around.

Our conversation is natural and light. We talk about school, plans for the future, hobbies, favourite sports teams, and the typical get-to-know-each-other topics. I study Liam and Chelsea's developing rapport through dinner, but I don't pick up on a romantic vibe at all. Isla, on the other hand, is looking at Liam like he hung the moon. She's captivated by each word he says and giggles like never before.

When we're all done eating, Zach and Isla snuggle together to watch a movie while Chelsea and Liam go back to work on their schoolwork. I clean up the dinner dishes with Bond's help before heading to my office to organize my schedule and notes for the upcoming week.

Lost in a world of family drama, trust issues, infidelity, and closeted sexuality, I scan through my notes to prepare myself for everything in store for me this week. Working on my own offers me a much wider variety of clients and, therefore, a wider variety of issues than I previously dealt with working only with children. My previous area of expertise leaned heavily toward consequences from abandonment, problems forming emotional attachments, and having no sense of security.

With all the people I have worked with over the last six years as a counsellor, I have realized that nearly everyone is battling something. We're all a little broken. That doesn't mean anyone is less worthy. As much as I struggle to see my own self-worth, I will continue doing this job for as long as I can, even when it's overwhelming, and help other people see their own value. Those who can't do, teach.

When I return to the living room, where I left Zach and Isla on the sofa watching a movie, I find Isla snuggling a sprawled-out Bond, and Zach is snoring on the floor. I'm not sure how that worked out, but I'm certain it's not normal for the dog to sleep on the couch while the human sleeps on the floor.

"Zach, Zach." I whisper as I shake his shoulder.

He doesn't budge. I shake him a few more times and he doesn't wake up, so my only choice is to leave him to wake up on his own. Isla hasn't dozed off yet, so I'm able to get her upstairs without having to carry her.

Upon arriving upstairs, Liam is just headed home. They inform me they've finished their schoolwork and he'll be back in the morning to pick Chelsea up. This carpooling works out so well. For the last few weeks, I haven't had to get out of my pyjamas before 9am.

After we perform Isla's bedtime routine, I tuck her in. I climb into bed myself, welcoming the soft sheets and quiet surroundings. My body practically melts into the mattress, and I realize how sore I am from the hours of cleaning today. I toss and turn for far too long until I hear quiet footsteps enter the room as the splinter of light from the doorway grows wider.

"You left me on the floor." Zach sounds genuinely upset.

"I'm sorry. You wouldn't budge when I tried to wake you. I knew you'd come up eventually."

He laughs, which makes me realize he was just teasing me. Here I was about to tell him I couldn't sleep without him, but I'll keep that information to myself. He climbs in and wraps his arms around me, pulling me close. His arms feel like home.

Home is safe.

The last few weeks have flown by with very few dog-related furniture casualties or excrement foot-treatments. We've made progress with Bond and Isla is sleeping all night, every night. There are no number of sofas I wouldn't sacrifice for that cause.

I'm currently in the waiting room of *South Muskoka Memorial Hospital*, awaiting the next special little person in my life. Quinn has been in labour for several hours, but I vacated the room so her mom could stay with her for a while. I have no expertise to offer. Her mother has at least been through the process twice before.

As I continue to pace back and forth, a red-eyed Tyler walks out carrying a tiny human wrapped in a hospital-issued, gender-neutral receiving blanket. Tyler is beaming like a proud father.

Tears start streaming down my face, as I am completely overcome with joy. I video call Zach so we can have this moment together, even from a distance. He stayed home with the girls so I could be here to focus on Quinn.

"Hey, Baby. Any news yet?"

I hold up my phone in selfie-mode, bringing Tyler and his little bundle of love into the frame. "Look who just arrived. A proud Daddy."

Tyler's already impossibly wide smile grows even more. "Hey, Trigger. I want you to meet someone." He holds the baby up so Zach and I can both see. "It's a boy. We have a son."

I squeal with delight, giving Tyler a side hug and gushing over my best friend's baby boy. He is absolutely perfect. He has a head of fine, dark hair, and his eyes are fairly alert considering the journey he's just been on.

"Congratulations, Buddy. He's perfect." Zach's eyes radiate happiness through the screen.

"What are you going to name him?" I ask. Quinn has been tight-lipped about baby names, and I'm eager to find out what they have chosen.

"Um. Well, I wanted to run something by you." Tyler's grin turns into a tight line, and his serious eyes focus on Zach through the miracle of modern technology. "We were thinking, if the baby was a boy, we would name him Leo."

Shock hits me, and I nearly drop my phone. I recover and study Zach's facial expression. He looks just as surprised as I am.

"Wow." Zach wipes a lone tear from his cheek. "I... I don't know what to say. I'd be honoured. Leo would have been honoured."

I look at baby Leo with so much love in my heart, knowing his namesake would have been so proud seeing his memory live on through this little man who is so adored.

"Leo Ezra Ochoa." Tyler stares at his son with a glint in his eyes that says more than 1000 words ever could. "Do you want to hold him, Auntie Zara?"

I'll love him, but holding him is a distinct challenge altogether. "Um, actually, I'd like to see Quinn. I want to see how she's doing." I sidestep the question because I am so nervous around babies. It's possible I'd drop him, so I definitely don't want to try while standing.

"Text me before you leave the hospital, okay Baby? Tell Quinn I said congratulations. I can't wait to teach the little guy how to throw a baseball since his dad was only second best on the team." Zach laughs at his own joke, which really is what makes it funny.

"Har, har, har. You're so funny. But I'm sure Leo will love throwing a ball around with his Uncle Zach."

I can tell by the expression on Zach's face that hearing the name Leo again is emotional for him. After losing his twin brother, Leo, to a drunk driver when they were only fourteen, Zach's life took a nosedive into misery for many years. His parents died in a household accident several years later, leaving twenty-one-year-old Zach scrambling to support his little sister Jasmine while he was in University, himself. The lengths he went to in order to make sure Jasmine was in a home where she was loved and cared for made me fall for him hard and fast. I know his family would be so proud of him if they could see him now.

Given that they all went to the same school, Tyler was as close with Leo as he was with Zach. After Leo died, and Zach's mother spiralled into depression, it was often Tyler and his family that helped to ensure Zach had everything he needed. As a result, their bond is much more than friendship—they are family.

I hang up the video call and walk down the hallway to the recovery room Quinn was transferred into. Her face lights up when she sees me, then she immediately starts crying—what I hope are tears of joy. These pregnancy emotions are killer to interpret. Maybe Zach is right about being able to skip this stuff.

"Chica!" Quinn cries.

"Congratulations, Mommy. How are you feeling?"

She uses the thin sheet she is covered with to wipe her tears. She's wearing the hospital gown I gifted her, looking like she just stepped out of a maternity photoshoot. You'd never guess she just shot a human out of her.

"He's so beautiful. I love him so much." Quinn's blubbering is adorable.

"He is beautiful. You did good."

"I can't believe I'm a mom! I have no idea what I'm doing." She sniffles and lets out a giggle.

I wish I had some helpful advice for her, but the truth is, I don't know what I'm doing either and have zero experience with boys or newborns. Eight months in, I haven't figured out this Mom-gig and I doubt I ever will. "You're going to be a great mom, Amiga. You just have to love him." I lean in to give my gorgeous friend a hug, hoping my emotions are interpreted better through our embrace than my words.

Quinn asks if I want to hold him, and I hesitate but agree after seeing the pride in her eyes. I take a seat in the pleather side chair that was clearly designed with sanitation in mind, not comfort, and Tyler walks toward me to place Leo in my arms. Once I'm confident I'm holding him securely, Tyler releases his son's head, and for the first time in my thirty years, I'm holding a newborn baby. I never even held my nieces or nephews until they were a few months old because I was afraid I would break them, so this is a totally new experience.

This brand-new human is going to change my best friend's life forever. I can't help but think how lucky he is to have Quinn and Tyler as parents. Little Leo's near-navy-blue eyes, miniscule eyelashes, and full cheeks have my useless ovaries jealous. He's utter perfection and is so content in my arms as his eyes grow heavy. He had a big day today and deserves his rest. With Quinn's approval, Leo falls asleep in my arms as I stare at him with complete adoration.

I summon all my will power to hand over Leo because I need to get home. It's late, and I'm sure mommy and daddy would like some alone time with their baby boy and be able to get some sleep of their own.

My arms are both asleep, so when Tyler gently lifts sleeping Leo from me, I stand up and feel like one of those inflatable firecracker-tube men used for promotions—arms flailing about with no rhyme or reason. Quinn is finally dozing off, and I don't want to wake her with my orangutan arms, so I whisper my goodbyes to Tyler and sneak out the door.

The distance to my car proved enough to wake my arms up and I'm ready to get home, so I text Zach to let him know I'm on my way.

Twenty minutes later, I arrive home. The house is quiet, and not even Bond comes to greet me. I assume everyone is in bed, so I make my way to the stairs. As I walk past the back door, I notice the outside light is on and I see movement.

My anxiety likes to play fun games in these situations—let's imagine all the ways Zara can die in a home invasion. We play this often, and I never win.

I sneak to the door to glimpse who or whatever is on our back deck. I never imagined I'd find what I do.

Zach is sitting on a patio chair, drinking a beer. That would be fine except it's January, and he rarely drinks.

"What are you doing out here? You're going to freeze."

His startled face looks up at me, but he doesn't speak. His eyes are bloodshot, and his nose is red. He's wearing only a sweater and sweatpants with his house slippers on his feet—he did not dress for Canadian winter.

"What's wrong?" I bend down in front of him, forcing him to look at me. "Zach, please answer me."

Still nothing.

I grab his hands and pull him up to stand, then lead him into the house. I feel like I'm dragging a zombie, which my brain adds to its database as a potential cause of death.

Once we're inside, I take him to the sofa, sit him down, and wrap us both in a fleece blanket. I rub my hands along his arms to warm him up and wait for him to speak. I wait. And wait. And wait.

I can't take the silence anymore. "Why were you sitting out in the freezing cold? Please, tell me what's wrong."

He releases a deep sigh, which is the first sound he's made since I arrived home. I'm comforted knowing aliens did not come and steal his voice box. "What if I can't save him?"

I peer at my soulmate, confused by his question. "Who? Can't save who?"

A tear slides down Zach's cheek. "Leo. What if I can't save him, either?"

My heart has an actual physical response to his words—causing me an unfamiliar pain. Zach has held onto so much guilt that he wasn't able to save his brother, but it was an impossible situation and he was unconscious himself. I pull him into my arms even tighter and try to comfort this broken man the best I can. "You couldn't have done anything for your brother. I know it's hard because you're an incredible man and you want to fix everything, but you can't."

He sobs. For the first time since I've known him, Zach is overcome with sadness that continues to pour out of his eyes. I can't help but cry with him. He feels broken in my arms and I never imagined the name Leo would bring him so much pain.

"I'm so sorry. You're the greatest man I know, and Leo would be proud of you."

"I couldn't save him. I couldn't save him."

For someone who works in the field I do, I'm lost in how to comfort the man I love. I wish I could tell him he can't feel guilty because it was the drunk driver's fault, but placing blame somewhere else will solve nothing. So, I hold him while he breaks in my arms. I try to hold him together, but I think he's held in his grief for so long, right now he just needs to fall apart.

After I don't know how long, Zach's breathing becomes calm and steady. He's fallen asleep on me, and I do not have the heart to wake him. For the second time tonight, I have a guy I adore sleeping in my arms, but this one is significantly heavier. Regardless, just like Leo needed loving arms to hold him earlier, I will hold Zach for as long as he needs.

Before the sun rises, Zach shoots up out of his sleep. "Oh no. I'm sorry, Baby."

I reach up to pull him back toward me, but my arms are two useless bags of bones, and my back has aged twenty years. My involuntary grumbles have Zach issuing multiple apologies.

"It's okay. My arms are just asleep."

He runs his hands over his face, then settles on the opposite end of the sofa, elbows on his knees and head in his hands. "I'm so sorry. I don't know what got into me."

Is he seriously feeling guilty for missing his brother? His *twin* brother? "Emotion. Emotion got into you, and it's fine. It's necessary. You were grieving."

"It's been eighteen years, Zara. I should be over it by now."

"No." My forcefulness startles him, but I don't let it deter me. "Don't you pull this macho crap or tell me you should be over it. That's probably *why* you were so emotional! Because instead of talking about things, you think it's been long enough, it shouldn't bother you anymore, so you suppress your feelings."

He opens his mouth to speak, but I cut him off.

"Grief is not a journey in one direction. What happened last night was an understandable turn in the other direction, but there's nothing to be sorry for. You love your brother. It's okay to be sad sometimes."

He glances at me, giving me a one-sided smirk. "If you say so, Miss Counsellor."

"It's *Mrs.* Counsellor, thank you very much, and I say so."

Zach dives on top of me, trapping me under the weight of his body. "I love you so much. I hope you know that."

"Yeah, I do. I don't understand why, but I believe you when you tell me."

Zach straightens his arms to raise himself to look at me. "I don't understand how you don't understand how amazing you are."

"Well, I don't understand how you don't understand how I don't understand."

"Ahem. Good morning." I hear Chelsea's voice from over near the stairs. The girl is going to have to wear a bell if this keeps happening.

"Good morning, girls." Zach says, which is met with a bark from Bond. "You too, buddy."

"Toe pile!" Isla shouts as she darts across the living room and dives on top of Zach's back.

We're quickly joined by Bond too, and suddenly, Chelsea is the only one left out.

"Get over here, Chels. Hop on!" I issue her an invitation, not expecting her to partake. After a second of hesitation, she comes barrelling across the room and jumps onto the pile.

"I think you mean 'toad pile,' Troublemaker," Chelsea says with the most amazing smile I've ever seen grace her face.

The giggling pauses for a moment. "Why would I say toad pile? None of us have toads."

We all burst out laughing, except Isla, who is genuinely confused. Our morning "toe pile" becomes one of the best moments of my life. We did not anticipate or plan it out like a trip to *Disney World*. It wasn't an elaborate production like a party. It was a spur-of-the-moment display of love between every member of our family, and I'm so overwhelmed with love and happiness, I feel like my face might rupture.

"I love you guys."

What was already on my list of top ten greatest moments of my life just skyrocketed to top five. "What?" My wide eyes stare at the gorgeous, smiling ginger on the top of our family stack.

"I love you guys," Chelsea repeats.

We have been living as a family for ten months. Granted, it took a few months before the paperwork was settled and we officially became a legal family, but that was a formality for me. I already knew nothing would stop me from giving these girls the best lives I could. But never once, in all the time that has passed, has Chelsea said those words to me. I can't help but cry happy tears.

"I love you so much, Chels. I love you all so much," I blubber. I'm full-on ugly crying with dripping snot and all.

"Chels. You broke Mommy."

We all laugh again—except Isla, so I reassure her. "No, Sweet Girl. These are happy tears."

She looks at me with her features twisted, still looking as cute as can be. "Why do people cry if they're happy?"

"Well, sometimes when we have a feeling so intense, it can overwhelm us. We cry for many reasons when our feelings get too big. When we're sad, happy, angry, scared. But I promise, these are happy tears."

"I hope I get to cry happy tears." Isla snuggles into Bond with her eyes closed and a smile on her face. She's found contentment.

I couldn't ask for more. "Me too, Sweet Girl. I hope the only tears you cry are happy tears."

As the long, Canadian winter drags on, life in the Haynes household has become more routine and less chaos. The girls both seem content and happy. School is going well for them both, and I couldn't be more proud of them.

Mine and Zach's one year wedding anniversary is next Thursday, so we've made plans to go to Toronto for the weekend, and Jasmine will stay with the girls, with my mom agreeing to check in or offer help as needed. The girls are both easy to manage and shouldn't offer any trouble, which makes leaving them less scary.

We arrive at our accommodations shortly after check-in time on Friday afternoon, intentionally planning the weekend before our anniversary to avoid the March Break rush. We're directed to our seventh-floor room, so we make our way up in the elevator, suitcase in tow. The premiere suite we'll be staying in is bigger than my previous condo, and features modern, clean décor and furniture. Zach spared no expense to make our weekend memorable.

We opted out of taking a honeymoon in order to adopt our girls after our courthouse wedding, so this is our first weekend away.

I don't know what Zach planned for the evening, but it's already five o'clock by the time we get settled in our room. We agree to visit the restaurant bar in the hotel. Having to drive anywhere downtown Toronto during Friday rush hour does not sound like a relaxing evening to me.

We arrive at the restaurant, and we're seated promptly. The atmosphere is very modern and clean. A bit too bougie for my taste, but I'll take it.

We're both scanning the menu, enjoying casual conversation, when I realize there are very few vegetarian options available. Rather than complain, I just ask for their soup and a salad. I'm going to be starving by midnight, but I stowed away some Oreos in our suitcase. My chronic over-packing often comes in handy.

After a mediocre meal, a conversation that we had to steer away from kid-related topics, and a few glasses of wine, we head back to our room. I haven't had alcohol since Quinn and Tyler's wedding eighteen months ago because of my anti-anxiety medication. Three glasses of wine have me toasted.

We stumble... correction, I stumble, Zach holds my arm and walks steady as a rock—a glorious, dreamy, handsome rock—into the elevator to go back to our room.

"I've never seen you drunk before. This weekend is starting out with a bang." He laughs.

"Now, now. Mr. Haynes. Don't be presumptuous." I press him up against the elevator wall and capture him with a kiss.

"I like drunk Zara."

"I hope you like sober Zara too, because this is a onetime thing."

"Then let's make the best of it. I'll love sober Zara later." He winks at me as the elevator doors open on the seventh floor and pulls me toward our room.

I cut our romantic encounter short when I blurt out, "We should call to check on the girls."

Zach, clearly disappointed by my request, tries his best to sweep my request off. "They're fine, Baby. Jas knows to call if there are any issues."

"Please, I just want to check on them."

After a frustrated sigh, Zach concedes, and he's calling Jasmine to check on everyone. As he said, everyone is fine, including Bond, who is currently watching *Air Bud* with Isla.

"See. Everything is fine. Just relax."

"Let's take a walk."

Zach is a patient man, but after I say those words, he looks miffed. "A walk?"

"Yeah. I think fresh air would be good to help clear my head. Then we can come back and warm up together."

Zach agrees, and we bundle up to go take in the sights and sounds of downtown Toronto. Alcohol really must have suppressed my anxious thoughts because on most days, I prefer to stay cooped up inside. Exploring the country's most populous city is way out of the realm of normal Zara behaviour.

The temperature is around three degrees, so it's cold but not bitterly. We stroll down York Street, popping in to a few open businesses along the way to browse and warm up before continuing on to *Harbour Square Park*.

We walk hand-in-hand, but Zach says little. I get the impression he's upset with me, and I don't blame him. I've been so focused on mom-mode, that I haven't been in wife-mode very often. It's not fair to him, and he deserves so much more than what I offer.

"Zach?" A melodic, cheerful voice interrupts my thoughts, and Zach drops my hand as he spins around.

"Averie. Wow. Hi. What are you doing here?" Zach steps forward to greet the stunning brunette goddess with a hug.

"I live just over there in the condos. What brings you here?"

I'm standing a few feet behind the interaction, waiting for my husband to introduce me to the beautiful woman before him. But he doesn't. He doesn't give me a second glance until several minutes later when she walks away with an exaggerated butt sway.

Averie, I learn from eavesdropping, is a model and does quite well for herself. She's single and hasn't dated anyone seriously since Zach, and apparently misses him "especially on frosty nights like tonight."

Zach turns around like he's just realized I was still there, eyes wide and mouth hanging open. If he had a marquee-ticker on his head right now it would read, 'You done messed up big time, mate.'

Without a word, I turn and start walking back to the hotel—a hotel I don't even want to go back to right now, but I have no other choice unless I want to bunk with one of the kind homeless folks who pepper the downtown core.

Zach walks along behind me, trying to make small talk as if he hadn't just forgotten I existed as soon as his ex-girlfriend/model entered the scene.

I ignore every word he says, continuing my pace down the crowded sidewalk, avoiding eye contact with pedestrians who cross my path. With each step I take, my self-worth sinks deeper and deeper. It's clear I was Zach's consolation prize and if given the choice, he'd choose Averie. Averie and Zach; love from A to Z. I can't compete with her.

"Zara, would you stop?" Zach calls from a few feet behind me.

No. I won't. I pick up my pace, because if I look at him, I'll burst out crying and my face will freeze.

"Baby, please. Stop so we can talk."

That does it. I spin around to look at him, and he nearly crashes into me while taking his own forward steps to catch up to me. "I'm not your 'baby', okay? I'm not even worth you introducing to your beautiful ex-girlfriend, who you're clearly still attracted to. I know I'm not worth much Zach, but it didn't occur to me I was some pity-prize." And the tears start. If I end up with frostbite on my face, becoming disfigured and even less attractive than I am, so help me, I will track Averie down with a weed-whacker.

Zach steps forward to wrap his arms around me, but I push myself away, using his hard chest as a launch pad and carry on my stomp back to the hotel. I walk through the lobby doors with Zach hot on my heels. I press the button for the elevator and stand off to the side with my arms crossed, tapping my foot on the gleaming charcoal marble floor.

When the sound indicates the elevator arrived, I step in, turning right inside the door. "You can take the next one." I glare at Zach, not wanting to be in his presence right now. I ignore the sadness in his eyes, press the door-close button, and rocket up to the seventh floor.

My fury is short-lived when I get to our hotel room door and realize Zach has the key. So, like a tantrum-having toddler, I lean back against the wall beside the door and wait. A few short seconds later, the next elevator opens, and Zach walks out with a facial expression that resembles a timid dog. I'd have sympathy for a dog, but I have none for him right now.

"Baby, please—"

"Nope. Open the door." I interrupt him. I've just dried my tears and reactivated my angry face.

I walk into the bedroom of our massive suite, collecting a pillow and blanket, and toss them onto the sofa for him. "You can sleep there." I point to the couch. "Or call Averie. I'm sure she'd be happy to let you in her bed for the night." I slam the bedroom door, leaving a barrier between me and the man I love. A physical barrier that represents the emotional barrier that developed in a split second.

I cried myself to sleep last night. I sobbed until I passed out, never allowing Zach to address what happened on our walk. If I had a pint of ice-cream, I would have drowned my sorrows in it, but I settled for wiping my mascara tears on 1000 thread-count Egyptian cotton sheets.

The water is running in the bathroom, so I know Zach is up, but I'm afraid to face him. I can't get beyond the feeling of worthlessness I'm drowning in, and I don't think anything he says can make it right. I stood behind him like I was a nobody while his ex-girlfriend shamelessly flirted with him, and he didn't even mention the fact that he's married. Seeing that interaction leaves me with a lot of doubts.

"Baby, can I come in?" Zach's hushed voice penetrates the door.

I don't think I'll ever be ready to talk about this, but unless I want to stay locked in this room until I die, I'm going to have to face him. I can't afford to stay here forever. "Fine."

The eyes that once mesmerized me with a simple glance look bloodshot and lifeless. Dark under-eye circles are obvious on his otherwise flawless face. He hasn't slept.

He starts with a simple apology. "I'm sorry about last night."

"Which part? Sorry for fawning all over your ex-girlfriend in front of me? Sorry for not acknowledging I existed? Sorry for neglecting to tell her you're married with two kids at home? Tell me, what *are* you sorry for? Sorry that I was even there and held you back from what you really wanted?"

"What? No! Of course not. Zara, I only want you. Averie… well, she's my past, but I wanted to keep her there."

"From where I was standing, it looked like you wished she was part of your present."

He walks over and climbs onto the bed beside me, staying overtop of the covers. "No. That's not it at all. Averie and I dated for two years, but I never felt like we were serious. She was trying to make it as a model, and basically used me as her default date to go to events. She would get angry if I couldn't attend somewhere with her, especially if it was because Jasmine needed me. Jas hated her, actually. I started noticing how jealous and possessive she became, so I ended it and never looked back." He releases a sigh. The look in his eyes tells me he's being honest. "She caught me off guard last night, and I didn't introduce you because she has a history of being petty and rude. I didn't want to give her the chance."

That's a new one. He didn't introduce me to his sexy model ex because he was trying to protect me? Right. Even though I believe he is telling the truth, I don't reply to his claims.

"I'm sorry I made you feel you were less important, Baby. I promise, it was the exact opposite. I barely had a second to think after she said my name, and my only thought was keeping you from ending up in her crosshairs."

I stay silent, still processing everything he's telling me. I want to trust him. Before last night, he's never given me a reason not to, even when his sexy secretary made regular advances toward him.

"Zara Haynes, you are my one and only, and I will protect you until my dying breath. Please believe me. I love you more than you'll ever know. Can you forgive me?"

After hearing him say that he was trying to protect me, I feel like I'm the one who needs to be forgiven. I thought I moved on from this blowing-things-out-of-proportion mentality, but it's a hard habit to break. There's only one path forward. "I'm sorry too."

Without another word, Zach leans in to kiss me, and suddenly our tickets for a matinee show at the *Princess of Wales Theatre* are nowhere on our minds. We spend the entire morning and better part of the afternoon becoming reacquainted with each other, taking a lesson forward that we need to trust each other to always have the other's best interests at heart.

Our evening starts with dinner at the top of the *CN Tower* in the *360* restaurant. We're given seats at a table for two away from the window. Not that it matters much as it's snowing and gloomy outside, so you can't see far, regardless. The atmosphere is intimate—and I don't mean between Zach and I. The tables are situated so closely together; it is not the place to have a strategy session if you're planning a bank heist. The counsellor in me has to avoid giving other couples advice who are seated around us as they complain about their friends and family. Romance 101: Don't spend your evening talking about your father-in-law's proctologist appointment.

Needless to say, the evening is decidedly un-romantic. We finish our meals and walk down the flight of stairs to the observation deck. The glass floor overlooking the city appears as nothing more than swirling snow beneath our feet, without even so much as one city light permeating the blizzard.

We opt to call it a night, heading 144 stories back down to the ground floor in the super-speed elevator. As luck would have it, the snow isn't so bad on street level.

Strolling down Bremner Boulevard toward our hotel, I notice a man staggering out of a bar, looking absolutely rat-arsed. He's alone, staggering across the sidewalk. I watch in horror as lights flicker on a black Mercedes and the man climbs into the driver's seat.

Zach shouts at me, "Call 911!" He runs over to the man's car and starts pounding on the driver's window. The man behind the wheel ignores Zach's presence and turns on the ignition.

As I see the puff of hot exhaust air meeting the cool air around it, I hear words from the other end of my phone, "911, what's your emergency?"

I relay to the dispatcher that we need police presence to deal with a drunk driver, and with a few questions, she's assured me officers are on their way.

My eyes can't tear away from the scene in front of me as Zach pleads with the man to shut the car off. He's trying to open the driver's door but having no luck. The brake lights turn on for a few short seconds, then turn off as the car lurches forward. Thanks to marvellous modern-day German engineering, the car gathers quite a bit of speed before crashing into the rear of the vehicle two parking spaces ahead. Evidently Mister Ratarse forgot to turn the steering wheel.

My first instinct is to check and make sure Zach is okay. He was safely out of the way on the sidewalk—well, he should have been safe, but the way this drunken buffoon drives, nobody was safe. Zach ran the twenty feet forward and pulled the driver's door open after unlocking it through the broken window. He's far more cordial with Mister Ratarse than he deserves, but that's because Zach is a compassionate man. He hates drunk drivers with a passion after one overturned his once happy life, yet he's still taking the time to make sure the man is okay rather than pulling him out on the sidewalk and pummelling the life out of him.

The police arrive on the scene moments later and they ask both Zach and I to give statements, which they take inside the establishment Mister Ratarse stumbled out of so we don't freeze.

Zach and I walk away toward our hotel after the police have thanked us for being decent citizens, immediately pegging us as 'out-of-towners.'

We don't speak a word for several hundred metres before I ask, "Are you okay?"

He stops walking. "I… I don't know. I should have done more."

What does he think he could have done? He obviously did more than many people would have and put himself at risk to stop the man's reckless actions.

I reach to take his hand. "You did all you could. No one was hurt, and he's under arrest now. It's out of your hands."

We walk slowly, with our hotel finally coming into sight.

"I guess."

"Come on. Let me show my hero how much I appreciate his bravery." I lead Zach through the lobby doors in a distinctly different manner than the night before. Tonight, he's not sleeping on the couch.

Our weekend doesn't go as planned, and we likely won't make another attempt at a romantic getaway weekend in Toronto anytime in the future, but we come home stronger than ever, reconnected and ready to face whatever life throws at us next.

Quinn and Tyler have invited our family on a camping trip to *Killbear*, so we can spend the May long weekend enjoying each other's company. Neither of our girls have ever been camping before, and I haven't been for a long time, so it's bound to be an adventure—especially with five-month-old Leo.

I've never been to *Killbear Provincial Park* before, but I've heard a lot about it. Naturally, when they asked us, I researched it to ease my anxiety. I wanted to make sure we're not required to kill bears, as if that were the price of admission. As a family of vegetarians, that would be a hard pass.

Zach rented a camping trailer for the weekend, so we don't have to worry about purchasing camping gear. For the girls' first trip, it wouldn't be practical, because they may hate it. Chelsea asked if Liam could join us, and Isla will bring Bond. Liam has been spending a lot of evenings and weekends at our house and he's become a part of the family. He and Zach have developed a friendship that may look strange to the rest of the world, but for our unconventional family, it's just how we operate.

As we're packing up the supplies we'll need into the pop-up trailer, I feel myself going over my mental and written checklists again. I don't want to be stuck in the bush, thirty minutes from civilization, without necessary items.

"Baby. We're going camping, not moving."

I look at Zach, deadpan. "Only you can prevent forest fires," I reply as I load a fire extinguisher in the trailer. I can't understand why he thinks it's excessive.

"Right. Anyway, I've got the cooler loaded up, so we just need to squeeze that in somewhere and we should be good to go." Zach walks toward me, placing his arms on either side of my head, trapping me against his vehicle. He leans in to give me a kiss. "We probably won't have another moment alone until we get back home. I don't know how I'll survive."

At that moment, Chelsea and Isla come bounding out of the house as Liam struggles to carry the loaded cooler. I chuckle because once again we've been interrupted, and Zach's dropped head tells me how he feels about it. I give him a quick peck on the cheek to hold him over.

The doors on the SUV are all open, including the tailgate. Because we're at capacity, Bond is going to have to ride in the trunk to the campground. It's him or Liam, and I'm not sure Mr. and Dr. Davis would appreciate that much.

The kids are all excited, and their energy is contagious. All the anxiety I am feeling surrounding a new, unknown adventure is slowly but surely replaced by the thrill of what lies ahead. I'm so excited to spend time with my best friend, the kids, and the love of my life, get in touch with nature, and have a weekend free from electronics and work.

The drive is only about ninety minutes, so we arrive shortly after check-in time at two o'clock. It takes a few attempts to back the trailer into position on our site in Harold Point. By the time we're parked, I'm ready to pack up and go home—or get a divorce.

We lucked out to book two sites side-by-side with the Ochoas, and on account of trees being cut down recently, it feels more like we are on one big, conjoined site. Quinn and Tyler arrive a short time later. They stopped on the way because Leo was crying. He doesn't like the car, so he is always sure to let them know.

Quinn and I greet each other with a hug while my girls gush over how handsome Leo is getting. Zach helps Tyler get his camper in a suitable position, and the men set off getting camp set up. I'm not a stickler for traditional gender roles, by any means, but today, I'm going to sit back and watch them work while I hold my best friend's adorable baby boy.

Once we've set up the camper, I step inside to evaluate our home for the next three nights. Each end has a queen bed, with the dinette area serving as another sleeping space. I'm not sure it even qualifies as a twin bed, but Liam says he doesn't mind. I work away, getting the sheets and blankets on the beds, moving our clothing into the trunk of the SUV so we can access it there rather than clutter the camper. I stock the small—rather, puny—fridge with some drinks and we're all set.

Bond isn't thrilled about the idea of being tied up because he can't stay next to Isla as she runs around. He's used to having freedom at home, so a six-foot leash must feel like an anchor. After an episode of relentless barking, we opt to leave him untied and keep the leash attached. I'm not a rebel, but I don't think our camping neighbours want to listen to Bond's complaining for the next three days. The good thing is, he's so in love with Isla, I can't imagine him going anywhere.

The afternoon passes without incident. Bond stayed put on our campsite, never wandering beyond the perimeter aside from when we took Isla to the playground and he joined us. There were some other kids at the playground when we arrived, and Isla hid behind my back rather than interacting with them for quite a while. Once another little girl named Zoey came up to introduce herself to Bond and give him an ear scratch, a common interest was established, and the two young girls played together for nearly two hours with Bond watching their every move.

Isla and Zoey make tentative plans to meet tomorrow at the beachfront after lunch so they can build a sandcastle. I'm thrilled Isla made a friend. With her social anxiety, and the fact she is homeschooled, she struggles to connect with other children her age. Her making a little friend and seeing it's not always scary makes the trip here worth every swelling bug bite I've received. Except maybe the ones on the bottoms of my feet.

We spend the evening around the campfire and the guys work as a team to make quesadillas on the BBQ. Quinn, Tyler and Liam aren't vegetarians, so it was the perfect option to accommodate everyone. Considering none of the guys cook very often, dinner turns out really well and we're all stuffed an hour later.

The temperature dropped quite a few degrees, so we're bundled in sweaters, trying to keep warm. Liam brings out a few small blankets from inside the trailer and hands them to us girls. Tyler serenades us with his acoustic guitar, and the way Quinn looks at him makes me confident she has forgiven him for the pain of childbirth. Tyler teaches Liam a few songs, and Chelsea watches attentively as her friend unashamedly attempts to learn a new skill with an audience.

I lean back in my chair to stare up at the stars and breathe in the cool evening air. I can't help but think how each star is beautiful on its own, but when they're together, the impact is magical; just like these people around me. Each is unique and appreciated in their own way, but when they're all together in front of me, they are a beautiful sight to behold.

Sandcastle building occupies a good portion of our day, along with playing at the dog beach with Bond, and touring the visitor's centre. After a late dinner, we agree to go chase a sunset.

All eight of us, plus Bond, hike along the steep, moss-covered red-granite rocks, weaving our way through the pine forest that offsets Harold Point. Tyler has Leo strapped in a baby carrier and the two of them are stuffed into an oversized bug jacket. We collectively smell like lemon and eucalyptus and look ultra-fashionable in our hats with bug-hoods and pants tucked into our socks.

With flashlights in hand, so we can find our way safely back out, we traverse the uneven ground in an effort to catch a magnificent view. We reach the peak and watch the sun set over Georgian Bay, in awe of the bright orange colours painting the sky. It appears as if the entire sky is ablaze with thick, dark clouds suspended over the fiery landscape. The air is thick, and the waves are violently crashing into the rocks below. It would be majestic if it weren't for the blackflies buzzing about and the deer flies circling us.

"It looks like we're going to get a storm tonight," Zach concludes as we watch the sun drop below our field of vision.

The thought makes me nervous. Spending the night in a pop-up camper with a storm on the other side of the canvas is not my idea of a good time. I hope the rental company waterproofed our temporary shelter sufficiently.

"I hope not. It's one thing if we're at home"—I scan the horizon, searching for a break in the cloud cover, to no avail—"but out here is a different story."

Zach chuckles, pulling me closer to place his arm around me. "Don't worry, Baby. I'll keep you safe." He winks at me, which I barely notice given the fading light. "And warm."

"Zach." I roll my eyes, which I'm sure escapes his notice. "I'm not worried about me. I want the kids to be okay." I look to see Isla in between Liam and Chelsea, holding each of their hands as they take in the fleeting colours of the sky. "Neither of them like storms."

"We'll be all right. What's the worst that can happen?"

I shoot him a glare so intense, not even darkness can hide it. "*Never* ask someone with anxiety that question."

"Right. Sorry. It will be fine. Don't worry." He cringes, knowing he shouldn't tell me not to worry, either. It's my only talent.

Despite the pesky insects, we enjoy our nature walk and arrive back to camp in the dark. Another evening around the campfire, roasting marshmallows, and listening to Liam pluck away at Tyler's guitar, has us all laughing and smiling. I haven't felt this relaxed for a long time. I can understand how people get addicted to camping.

Our conversation for the evening wraps up after discussing our own individual weather predictions, and we make our way into our trailers as the rain starts. We cram five bodies and a dog into our house on wheels; it feels cozy. Zach and I are sleeping to the left and the girls to the right. Liam is making do with the folded down dinette seat and the four-inch cushions squeezed together to resemble a mattress. He hasn't complained, but I feel bad he's spending his weekend developing back pain. We'll have to find a different solution for next time.

I don't know how much time passed, but I'm jolted awake by a crack of thunder that sounded as if it were directly overhead. Bond is whimpering, and Isla is trying to comfort him. Rarely does this scenario play out—usually the comforting is coming from Bond.

"It's okay. We're safe in here," Isla's soft voice tells her loyal companion.

"Isla, are you two okay?" I ask in a whisper-shout so she can hear my voice across the trailer amongst the sound of the rain pounding the outside.

"Bond is scared, Mommy. He doesn't like the storm."

I remember I purchased a Thundershirt for Bond when we first adopted him, but he hasn't needed it at home. Zach may have commented on my excessive packing, but right now, I'm grateful that I came prepared. The anxiety-aid is in Bond's suitcase, which is out in the back of the SUV. I have to help, so I use the key fob to unlock our vehicle, grab my raincoat and run outside in my pyjamas to find what I need.

As I'm digging through our gear, cursing myself for packing so much, I hear something that will haunt me for the rest of my life.

Isla releases a blood-curdling scream. "Bond! No!"

I pull my torso out of the car just in time to see a furry body run into the bush.

No. No. No. No. Please, no.

Bond is missing. He was so terrified by the thunderstorm, he ran into the middle of it. I can't believe I was stupid enough to not latch the door. I'm so overwhelmed with guilt, but I'm trying to suppress the self-hatred and focus on the task at hand.

At first light, we're all geared up to go on a search for him with whistles, leashes, and fully charged phones. Our first stop is at Zoey's campsite to ask if any of her family saw Bond, but no such luck. They offer to pitch in and help search for him. Within an hour, most of the campers have all banded together to help us search. If I wasn't already on the verge of tears because of our missing dog, I would cry because their generosity is so touching.

Isla is trying her best to search, but she's sobbing, terrified she's lost her best friend forever. We've all tried to comfort her and offer reassurance, but only one thing is going to make her feel better right now.

Liam and Chelsea have gone off to look around Lighthouse Point. The Ochoas are searching Granite Saddle. Our camping neighbours are scouring Harold Point. Zach, Isla and I are combing through the remaining campgrounds with the help of the park rangers, who have offered to ask other campers to keep their eyes open for our dog.

The primary concern is that the area is so dense with forest, which obviously means a lot of wildlife. Bond isn't a little dog, but he still could be in danger. I don't even want to think about the possibility of us not finding him. He may have been a challenge at first, but he's been nothing short of a loving, loyal sidekick for Isla.

After hours of searching, Zach and I insist on going back to our campsite to have something to eat and regroup with the others. Maybe if we switch our search areas, we'll all have renewed vigour and will have better luck finding Bond. Isla is reluctant to stop searching.

"Sweet Girl, we have to make sure you get something to eat. Bond wouldn't want you to starve. He might even find his way back to our campsite."

She tries to reply to me, but I can't understand her words through her tears. My child is heartbroken, and I feel helpless to fix it. I look at Zach with tears in my own eyes, only to be met with a solemn expression showing he feels the same way.

We arrive back at our campsite after texting the others, and everyone looks defeated. Chelsea's face is red and patchy, and Liam has his arm draped around her. Quinn looks more frazzled now than she did after giving birth, and I become overwhelmed with guilt for causing everyone so much stress. Leave it to me to ruin the best weekend we've all had in recent memory.

Zara, the screwup. At your service.

We've spent a full fourteen hours searching for Bond, with no sign of him. The park is a massive eighteen square kilometres and I feel like we've searched every inch. I collapse onto the bed inside the trailer, needing a moment to myself. For the first time since this ordeal began, I allow myself to feel. Tears pour from my eyes in a relentless stream, and after a few moments, I'm struggling to catch my breath. It's been over a year since I had a panic attack, but I feel like I have no control over the hysteria consuming me.

I hear the offending door unlatch and a pair of handsome green eyes peek in.

"Oh, Baby." Zach rushes over to me, pulling me into his arms. "It's okay. It will be all right."

I shake my head. "No. It's not all right. Nothing about this is okay. I exist solely to ruin everything. I… I can't do this anymore."

"What are you talking about? You haven't ruined anything. What can't you do?" I can see the concern in Zach's eyes, but at this moment I'm so angry with myself for adding nothing but upset to the lives of the people I love. I am only focusing on saving them from myself.

"This." I wave my hands around dramatically.

"Camping? That's fine. We don't have to ca—"

"No. Being responsible for a family. Every time I think I'm doing something good, I turn it into misery. I'm not cut out for this, and I'm sick of ruining everyone's lives."

Zach doesn't respond. He looks like he's going to vomit.

"I don't know what to do anymore." I sob as I collapse onto Zach's shoulder.

His gentle hand rubs my back as he holds me tight with his opposite arm. "I know today was a hard day, but I need you to listen to me. You have made our lives infinitely better. Don't think you haven't made my life worth living. Baby, I need you.." He raises my head with a finger under my chin so he's looking into my eyes. "I love you, Zara. We'll find Bond, and this will just be another thing we've overcome together."

My incoherent sobs make it impossible to reply. I would argue with him if I could speak, but I get the impression I wouldn't get anywhere.

The door clicks again, so I look up to see who is walking in on my meltdown. Isla.

"Mommy. Are you okay?" Her eyes are bloodshot and wide as she inches toward me.

"I'm okay, Sweet Girl." I feign confidence in words I have little in.

"I guess your sad feelings got too big."

"Yeah, they did." Her observation makes me feel even worse. "I'm sad Bond is missing, and I'm sad you're sad."

"I'm tired, and I miss Bond." Tears spring from her eyes as she climbs up on the bed beside Zach and me.

"I know. I'm so sorry. You can sleep with me tonight, and we'll look for him again tomorrow."

We're scheduled to leave tomorrow in the afternoon. Zach is due to be back at work Tuesday morning and we have to return our trailer rental, so we can't delay our departure. I don't even want to think about what we'll do if we have to leave before we find Bond. Or worse—what we'll do if we never find him.

The evening is marked with random bouts of crying and complete exhaustion. We don't even have the energy to cook, so Zach, Tyler and Liam go on a trip to a nearby restaurant to grab dinner and ask to hang up a handmade "lost best friend" sign Isla made that includes Zach's phone number. When they return, we eat in relative silence before retreating into our trailers for much-needed sleep.

Zach is on his own in the far bed while the girls have both snuggled in with me. Liam is the only one who doesn't have alternative sleep arrangements, though Zach offered him the bed.

Isla's sleep is fitful, with her thrashing, yelling, and crying. She's reverted to the night terrors she was having months ago—before Bond entered her life. Despite my best efforts to hold her and comfort her as she sleeps, she barely stays still and quiet for twenty minutes at a time. None of us get much rest.

When the birds start chirping, we all decide to get up, since no one was really sleeping, anyway. We have showers and get ourselves prepared for another few hours of searching before we have to pack everything up and leave.

Our thorough, five-hour search turns up empty. We return to our campsite defeated and depressed. Zoey comes running down the dirt road when she sees us return and gives Isla a hug. They may never see each other again, but the impact Zoey had on Isla will be felt far into the future. Zoey's mom Beth and I exchange email addresses so the girls can be digital pen pals and we can update them on our dog search. They spent a good portion of their "relaxing weekend" searching for a dog they didn't know for over twenty-four hours. They're good people.

Isla cries on her new friend. "He's gone. He's not anywhere."

Zoey is probably the first person to say what we're all thinking. "I hope he didn't get eaten by a bear."

Kids.

Isla releases Zoey to flash her a horrified look and starts crying even harder. I suppose this is why she prefers friendships with animals; they don't speak their minds.

"We'll come back in a few days and keep looking for him. The park has our phone numbers, there are a few posters up around the park, and Bond has a microchip if anyone finds him. We've done all we can for now." Zach, ever practical, tries to offer some reassurance to Isla and lets her know we aren't giving up.

Wednesday morning, I don't even want to get out of bed. I have sunk so deeply into depression, even my medication can't pull me out. I can't stop the relentless feeling that I ruin everything I touch.

Zach has gone to work, and Chelsea left for school, making it appear as if it's a normal day, but it's not. Isla and I are curled up in bed, worn out from crying and scanning lost dog groups online.

Quinn has been making phone calls to anywhere in the *Killbear* area she can get a hold of and has some friends from Parry Sound trying to spread the word too. I'm grateful for the help, but I feel hopeless.

I can't help but worry about how scared Bond must be. I know he spent months as a stray when he was a puppy, but it's been nearly a year since he hasn't had a warm bed to sleep in and food on demand. Not to mention he is probably stressed about the distance from Isla. All because I didn't latch the door.

I've cancelled my clients for the week and given Isla the day off from school again today. We'll probably eat ice cream and Oreos for breakfast, because as a mother, it's my duty to teach my girls how to handle heartbreak. This is an important life lesson, so her curriculum can wait.

We lie on the couch—the couch we own because of Bond's redecorating—and watch the first movie we can find that doesn't have a dog, *The Incredibles*. I wish I could be as brave and fearless as Elasti-Girl, but even she has her moments as a mother where she falls short. That's oddly comforting knowing a fictional cartoon character also has flaws.

It's past lunchtime and I haven't heard from Zach, which is odd. Normally, he calls to check in when he has a moment. Anxiety immediately makes me think of reasons he hasn't called, so to ease my mind, I call him. No answer.

I take a second to shake off the next round of anxious thoughts before dialling the number for his office. No answer.

Tammy, Zach's new receptionist, always answers the phone. Even when she's on her lunch break, she sets the phone to ring in Zach's office so no calls are missed. This is really unnerving.

I call Zach's phone again but get no answer and it doesn't go to voicemail. I send him a flurry of text messages, begging for confirmation he is still alive. No answer, and the messages go unread.

Isn't this just great? Now I have a missing husband in addition to the missing dog.

"What's wrong, Mommy?" Isla asks as we're snuggled on the couch together.

"Nothing. I was just trying to call Dad, but he must be busy."

She accepts my answer and goes back to watching the super-powered family defeat the fame-hungry villain.

I try to focus on the movie, but my thoughts are elsewhere.

My phone buzzes several minutes later, so I fumble to read the new message.

Zach: Sorry, Baby. Busy today.

I'm not sure how to take that. He's normally willing and eager to talk with me, so brushing me off like that has me concerned.

My brain is doing what it does best; creating every scenario that explains his aloof reply. He's cheating on me. He doesn't love me anymore. He's fed up with me ruining everything. I suppose he could be busy, but he's always made time for me before, even on his busiest days.

To distract myself, I start stress cleaning. I'm losing everything, and my world is crashing down around me. Our house felt like a home with Bond here. Since he's been gone, it just feels like a house with four sad people.

I hear nothing from Zach for hours. I've cleaned every room in our four-thousand square foot house, crying at every rogue tumbleweed of German shepherd hair I came across.

Just as I'm about to go online to check lost dog groups for the eighty-seventh time today, I hear our garage door open. Anxiety tells me that someone mugged Zach, stole his phone, and is now coming to claim our house as their own.

Seconds later, the door from the garage flies open, and in gallops a shaggy-looking canine and my gorgeous knight in shining armour.

"Bond!" Isla screams as she jumps off of me and runs toward her precious pooch. She collapses on the ground, wrapping her arms around him as he flops onto his back beside her.

My thoughts haven't quite caught up with what is happening yet until I look at Zach's face to see him beaming and Chelsea happily standing to his left.

"How did you… Where did… How…?" I can't form a full sentence.

"I got a call this morning, so I closed the office for the day and went to get him. He was found at the *Parry Sound Golf and Country Club*. One of their maintenance crew was out cutting the grass early this morning and saw Bond walking down the middle of the sixth fairway. This little guy travelled nearly thirty kilometres, which explains why we couldn't find him."

I look down at the floor to see Isla crying harder than she ever did when he was lost. The relief and sheer joy are so overwhelming in this moment, it's obvious how much Bond means to her.

Chelsea crouches down on the ground beside the two reuniting besties. "Are you okay, Troublemaker?"

Isla is sobbing, unable to stop the flow of tears and snot flowing from her face. She uses her sleeve to wipe her nose. "It's okay, Chels. These are happy tears."

My own floodgates open and happy tears spring from my eyes. Zach strides over to give me a hug, and I'm completely overwhelmed. Our family is back together; we're whole again. Our two beautiful girls, our dog, and the most perfect partner a girl could ever ask for. I might be broken, but my family has pasted me back together like a magnificent mosaic, reinforcing my every crack.

Maybe I won't get a 'happily ever after.' Maybe life will always have its trials that teach us to appreciate the ride. But I have learned to accept the 'happily right now.'

I'll just keep loving them.

THE END

If you enjoyed Zara's story, please consider leaving a review on Amazon and/or Goodreads. Your reviews help give me feedback so I can continue to learn, and also helps my books garner more attention from other readers. I would greatly appreciate your thoughts!

Don't forget, all proceeds from this publication are donated to Carter's Forever Rescue and Sanctuary. If you have other dog-loving readers in your life, consider gifting them a copy or make a donation to a dog rescue in your area.

To easily access links to my books, visit linktr.ee/burdenofproofreading. You can also sign up for my newsletter and find my social media links there.

Thank you, my Sweet Girl, Linaya, for another beautiful addition to the story.

Thank you to Lucia, Desirea, Dianne, and Harriet for beta reading in a crunch to meet my ridiculous self-imposed deadline. I appreciate you all for helping me do the Haynes family justice and for loving them as much as I do.

Of course, I can't neglect to mention my husband and children for their endless support and helping me complete these crazy projects I dream up. Being able to publish stories that my kids have been involved with has been such a blessing.

Also, to everyone who has picked up any of my books so far and sent me messages or left a review, you'll never know how much your words mean to me. I've been blown away by the feedback about my words resonating with you. It's the biggest compliment, and I'm humbled by each one of you.

First, I need to thank the wonderful people at Carter's Forever Rescue and Sanctuary. Not only for allowing me to write this book in their honour, but for doing the incredible work they do. Each day, I'm overjoyed seeing reports of dogs being adopted and sent off to live a life full of love and adventure. Your work adds love to the world, and that's not something to be overlooked. Visit them online at www.cartersrescue.com.

To the lovely folks at Mullins Pet Market for agreeing to be featured in this story. They really do have macrame leashes with tassles. They have the most amazing animal products that are sure to keep your fur baby happy. You can visit them online at www.mullinspetmarket.ca.

Lastly, thank you to Caitlin Bangsund for letting me include Marvellous Macey, The Delightful Days. Please, go read this book about this real life superhero. Find Caitlin's books online at www.caitlinbangsund.com.

Also By This Author:

You Are Enough Series:
We're All a Little Broken: Book 1 (Zara's story)
We're All a Little Overwhelmed: Book 1.5 (Zara's Extended Epilogue. All proceeds donated to Carter's Forever Rescue and Sanctuary.)
We're All a Little Guarded: Book 2 (Chelsea's story)
We're All a Little Tired: Book 2.5 (Chelsea's Extended Epilogue. All proceeds donated to SickKids Hospital.)
We're All a Little Scared: Book 3 (Isla's story)
We're All a Little Determined: Short Story Collection (Zach, Liam, and Theo's perspectives – available only in paperback or via BookFunnel. Find the link at linktr.ee/burdenofproofreading)

This women's fiction series focuses on various aspects of mental health and overcoming trauma. It addresses anxiety, depression, panic disorders, miscarriage, adoption, grief and loss, racism, discrimination, and more, but in a light hearted way that will also make you laugh. The entire series is set in Muskoka/Bracebridge, Ontario.

Visit my website to find coordinating journal and planners.

Suburban Watchdogs: Long-time friends, Justin, Morrie, Brendon, and Josh, live in a small farming town north of the big city. When crime starts making its way onto their streets, the group of men brought together by circumstance, rather than choice, band together to keep their town safe. One movie night watching a good ol' gangster film is all they need to motivate them to take action, thereby forming the Suburban Watchdogs. If criminals think they can just waltz into the Suburban Watchdogs' territory without resistance, they are mistaken.

Justin takes matters one step further by adopting Karma. Karma is a... female dog, and she'll make sure you get what's coming to you.

Join the group of unlikely friends and their canine companion on their hilarious vigilante mission and laugh at the chaos and mayhem that ensues.

<u>A New Leash on Life Series:</u>
Coming Spring, 2022
This series will consist of sixteen interconnected standalone romantic comedies. Some characters from Suburban Watchdogs and the You Are Enough series will have cameos or their own starring role!

Sign up for my newsletter or follow me on social media to learn more.

Linktr.ee/burdenofproofreading